Ride The Wind

Ride The Wind

Sandra Lott

Your New Life Ministries LLC

Contents

I want to thank Atty. James R. Snell Jr. for taking the time to assist me. I want to thank him for the information I needed regarding Criminal Domestic Violence (CDV), the laws that pertain to it, and the sentences that the varied charges associated with it carry.

I want to thank him as well for the book he sent regarding CDV, called Challenging CDV. It was very helpful and informative.

I would also like to thank Sister Kimberly Marie Hartfield of Go Fish Ministries Inc., whom I received psychological counseling information from to guide me in the counseling and healing process for the character in this book. Thank you for your assistance in helping me through a Christian perspective, which was the purpose of writing this book. It is to help the ones reading this who have been through or are now going through abuse similar to the character's experience, and to receive a revelation of the love of God.

God loves them and wants to heal them, and deliverance and victory is awaiting them through the loving arms of our Savior.
Thank you, and May God bless you both!

Preface

Ride the Wind is a story about Grace Thompson and how she finally learns to trust God. Through the abuse she suffered in her childhood and a storm-ridden marriage to an alcoholic and abusive husband, Grace comes to the end of herself. She has lost all hope in having any kind of life free from abuse. With the help of her younger sister, she finally cries out to God. In looking to God for one more chance at having a life of happiness, she discovers how to trust God and Ride the Wind of His love.

Whoever dwells in the shelter of the Most High will rest in the shadow of the Almighty. I will say of the Lord, "He is my refuge and my fortress, my God, in whom I trust." Surely he will save you from the fowler's snare and from the deadly pestilence. He will cover you with his feathers, and under his wings you will find refuge; his faithfulness will be your shield and rampart. You will not fear the terror of night, nor the arrow that flies by day, nor the pestilence that stalks in the darkness, nor the plague that destroys at midday. A thousand may fall at your side, ten thousand at your right hand, but it will not come near you. Psalms 91:1–7

Introduction

Ride the wind along with Grace Thompson and discover the overwhelming love of God as she did, and learn how to trust that God "will never leave you nor forsake you."

As a little girl, Grace was happy and carefree. She had beautiful long, brunette, curly hair and a smile that seemed to brighten up every room she walked into. Light glowed from within her—until everything changed; and that light was snuffed out.

Grace was abused sexually by her father, physically abused by her mother, and later in life, she was physically, as well as emotionally abused by her husband. The happy, carefree Grace became subdued; and darkness filled her heart, which was made up of despair, hopelessness, shame, and worthlessness. Grace became leery of everyone, believing in her heart that she could trust no one.

Everyone wanted to either use her or hurt her. Grace despised life itself and had tried, unsuccessfully, to commit suicide. There was no hope left within her, until one day, Lily entered her life. The Hebrew name for Lily is Shoshan, and it means "whiteness" and is a symbol of purity and resurrection. Through the unconditional love of Lily, the Lord would use her to help bring deliverance to Grace. Grace was about to be resurrected from a life of not trusting anyone, or even knowing who God is, to a life of undying love – a complete turnaround.

As Grace slowly takes one step of deliverance at a time. She discovers what it is like to be free and to be able to live and make decisions on her own without being afraid of getting abused.

God made a way for Grace and Jolisa, the younger sister from whom she had been separated for so long, to be together. It was Jolisa who introduced her to Jesus; and hope filled her heart for the very first time. Light began to glimmer in her eyes, as she learns the true meaning of her name.

Could there be complete healing for Grace? Grace begins to have hope. The Greek word for Grace is Charis meaning *"Grace, as a gift or blessing brought to man by Jesus Christ; favor; gratitude; thanks; kindness."*

When Grace begins to wonder, *who me, a blessing? Wow! How can that be?* This is the true beginning of her road to healing. Man can offer you a temporary peace, but God is Spirit, and his peace is eternal.

"For to us a child is born, to us a son is given, and the government will be on his

shoulders. And he will be called wonderful counselor, mighty God, everlasting Father, Prince of Peace" Isaiah 9:6.

If you have endured anything similar to the abuse that Grace suffered, then cry out to God and ask him to show you who he is and know that he is real and has a plan for your life.

"So I say to you: Ask and it will be given to you; seek and you will find; knock and the door will be opened to you" Luke 11:9.

The Lord was beaten and crucified for us, and by his stripes, we are healed.

"Surely our griefs he himself bore, and our sorrows he carried, yet we ourselves esteemed him stricken, smitten of God, and afflicted. But he was pierced through for our transgressions, he was crushed for our iniquities; the chastening for our well-being fell upon him, and by his stripes we are healed. All of us like sheep have gone astray, each of us has turned to his own way; but the Lord has caused the iniquity of us all to fall on him" Isaiah 53:4–7.

How great is his love. There is none greater than someone who would endure all that, though they did nothing wrong. He endured all the rejection, the cursing, the beatings, the thorns on his head, and the crucifixion to die in our place. There is no greater love than that.

"Greater love has no one than this: to lay down one's life for one's friends" John 15:13.

Travel along the road to healing with Grace and see the deliverance God has in store for her. Discover for yourself, as Grace discovers, a God who is love; and allow him to reveal the love he has for you through the path of restoration he leads her on. As God reveals himself to Grace and the love he has for her becomes alive and real, take that into your heart and receive it for yourself. For God is "no respecter of persons."

What he did for one he will do for all.

"So Christ was sacrificed once to take away the sins of many, and he will appear a second time, not to bear sin, but to bring salvation to those who are waiting for him" Hebrews 9:28.

God loved us and had a plan for our salvation before Jesus ever came. The Old Testament in itself is his story; it symbolizes and leads us straight to Jesus. You do not have to clean up to come to Jesus; just come. And he will do the rest. While mankind was sinning so greatly, God still loved us and had a plan, and he brought it to pass through Jesus Christ, our Lord.

"But God demonstrates his own love for us in this: While we were still sinners, Christ died for us" Romans 5:8.

Discover God's love for yourself along with Grace, and as God reveals himself to her, allow that same love to sink into your heart. You are loved.

"For great is your love, reaching to the heavens; your faithfulness reaches to the skies" Psalms 57:10.

Before you were born, he knew you and had a plan for every situation in your life. He has plans for good times and plans of restoration for the times people chose to ignore him and hurt you anyway. Trust God with your heart, and allow his perfect love to heal your heart.

"For you created my inmost being; you knit me together in my mother's womb. I praise you because I am fearfully and wonderfully made; your works are wonderful, I know that full well. My frame was not hidden from you when I was made in the secret place, when I was woven together in the depths of the earth. Your eyes saw my unformed body; all the days ordained for me were written in your Book before one of them came to be. How precious to me are your thoughts, God! How vast is the sum of them! Where I to count them, they would outnumber the grains of sand— when I awake, I am still with you" Psalms 139:13–18.

Oh, the joy that fills Grace's heart as the Lord heals it and deliverance finally comes! No more pain, no more despair, and no more shame! No more hopelessness and anger and no more fear! Grace has been set free! "Whom the Son sets free is free indeed."

As Grace walks the beach of her new home in Myrtle Beach, South Carolina, she remembers what she went through. She remembers the path of healing God led her on and the people He placed in her path along the way to be His feet, His hands, His voice, and His heart.

She remembers the joy and peace that filled her heart—the same peace she feels today. His peace is forever in her heart. The Holy Spirit of Jesus Christ dwells in her heart, and she has the strength to overcome any trial and knows he is there eternally and "will never leave her nor forsake her." His strength and his love carry her through life, and his joy radiates through her heart. She once felt overwhelming despair and shame and felt the sentence of death in her heart, and now she feels as if she can ride the wind—ride the wind of God's everlasting Grace. Ride along with Grace and discover it for yourself!

No lion will be there, nor will any vicious beast go up on it; these will not be found there. But the redeemed will walk there, and the ransomed of the Lord will return and come with joyful shouting to Zion, with everlasting joy upon their heads. They will find gladness and joy, and sorrow and sighing will flee away. Isaiah 35:9–10.

God's Abounding Love

Grace is: the act of God's unending abounding love for us.

Grace is: Understanding when we don't deserve it. Mercy and compassion, when we don't deserve it.

Grace is: Supplying all our needs and the strength that He gives us when we are weak.

By God's Grace: We have Joy and Peace in our hearts where pain and sorrow once dwelt.

By God's Grace: We have Forgiveness of all our sins when we don't deserve it.

By God's Grace: We are Victorious!

Grace is: The showing of God's love; when we are hurting, when we doubt Him; and when we sin against Him.

By God's Grace: We have eternal life, through Jesus Christ our Lord.

Grace is: Calvary and a love everlasting.

God's Grace

Your Grace is sufficient for me. I am not always abounding with joy and my faith seems to take a giant-sized nosedive.

But, there is something that I am always aware of and will always declare, Your Grace is sufficient for me.

I sometimes stumble and fall and detour from your path. Your Grace is sufficient for me.

Always at my side, walking beside me, is where you are, listening for my call. Your Grace is sufficient for me.

When I finally call out your name, the fear and pain in my heart goes away. The light of your love opens my eyes and your faithfulness I see, as your love fills me with joy and peace. Your Grace is sufficient for me.

Once again, your word becomes alive in me. Walking beside me, you will always be. Your Grace is sufficient for me.

1

Looking Back

It was a beautiful day; the sun was shining, but not too hot, and there was a slight breeze in the air. On days like this, Grace loved to walk along the beach. Her love of the beach is why she moved to Myrtle Beach—that and her new job. She has a cozy house, right on the beach and a covered deck facing the water. She loves to sit and stare out at the waves coming in, as she drinks her morning coffee. Grace used to live in Columbia, SC, but there were too many memories there, and for her, the beach always had a serene feeling to it. It instilled calmness into her spirit when she was there.

It was early, and the beach was fairly empty. It was the beginning of fall, and all the vacationers were gone, which is why the beaches were vacant. Grace loved this time of year. The air had a slight coolness but was not cold, and the different colors of the leaves, as they changed from green to red, orange, and yellow, were breathtaking. There were only a few people out jogging or walking along the water's edge, and it was quiet. It was Grace's favorite time of day.

Grace was young, only twenty-eight, but with the trauma she had been through and learned from and the wisdom from the Holy Spirit when she spoke, you would think she was a little more advanced in age. As Grace walked along the beach with her long, wavy, brown hair and thin white sundress blowing gently in the breeze, you could see the peace that radiated from her face. She loved this time of the morning when people were scarce along the beach. It was quiet and very peaceful. She loved to walk along the water's edge in her bare feet and feel the water and the sand run through her toes, as the waves rolled in from the sea. She felt free as she walked with the water splashing on her feet and the wind on her face.

She could also feel God's presence in a strong way. She prayed, "It seems like forever since I found you, Father, and you delivered me from all the abuse and healed my heart. Thank you so much! I feel so free inside as if I can ride the wind that is gently blowing across this beach. Thank you, Father, for never giving up on me."

******

As Grace continued walking down the beach, her mind drifted back in time to a period full of pain and fear; she went back to her childhood.

At four years old, Grace Williams was a happy little girl and she loved her mom and dad. She had long, curly, brunette hair and a smile that could melt the hardest heart. She lit up the room when she entered it. Her mom stayed home to take care of her and her baby sister, Jolisa. Jennifer, Grace's mom, had beautiful long brown hair just like Grace. Her dad's name was Mark. They were a happy family

Things changed one day when her dad lost his job at the paper mill in Charleston. As much as they loved Charleston and living close to the beach, he could not find any work. He had a friend in Columbia, who said he could get him a job working for the construction company he worked for, so they packed up and moved to Columbia.

They were sad as they packed up, but Mom made the best of it and said, "Grace, this will be an adventure, and you will get a brand new room."

It didn't seem like an adventure to her; she loved her room and her walks on the beach with her mom.

They found a house to rent in a part of town called West Columbia. It was a small house, but at least it was a home, and Grace had her own room again. The job went well with her dad at first, but after a few months, things got bad. Her dad started coming home late, and at the time, being so young, she did not understand why. Grace just knew that things were changing, and she did not like it. It made her mom sad, and her parents argued a lot when he came home at night.

She could remember her dad coming into her room at night to kiss her good night, and the smell of him made her sick. She didn't know what that smell was then, but she knew now; it was the smell of beer and cigarettes. Her dad was going out with the guys after work, and it became a habit. The more he went out, the more her parents argued, and the more they argued, the angrier and angrier her dad became. He felt as if he had a right to go out with his friends. After all, he was the one working hard all day.

The alcohol and bad mood affected his work, and one day his boss corrected him in front of everyone about leaving a board with nails sticking out of it in plain sight. Mark was in one of his moods because he and Jennifer had an especially bad fight the night before. Mark snapped. He shot his mouth off at his job, which cost him his job. He was ordered off the site, and that was that he had no job.

He came home late that night, falling down drunk, and had a bad mood to go along with it. He blamed Jennifer for everything. They got into another bad fight, and he slept out on the sofa.

Things did not get better, and he went from job to job after that. The drinking got worse. Mark and Jennifer seemed distant, and to make matters worse, Grace was about to be brought into it. Her dad would come home in his drunken state and sit on Grace's bed at night to kiss her good night and he had started touching her in areas that felt uncomfortable. She tried to make him stop, but he wouldn't and he treated her as if she was a woman instead of a child, and his own at that! She did not understand what was going on, and she was scared.

She was five now and still too young to understand the problems between her parents. She knew that her dad was different now. It was as if this man in her daddy's body was not her dad at all. When he left her room each night, she cried and cried. She wondered why he would do those awful things to her, and what she had done to deserve this happening to her. At only five years old, she knew it was wrong and felt as if she had done something. She felt ashamed.

Her daddy told her he would spank her well if she told anyone, especially her mom. The happy little Grace was now gone, and Jennifer could sense that something was wrong. Grace was having nightmares and was not sleeping well and had also become withdrawn. Grace was not playing with the other children as she used to, and was not eating very well either. Jennifer watched and studied Grace. She could tell something was not right by the way she avoided her dad. Even when he did happen to be home and sober.

Then one night, right after Grace's seventh birthday, Jennifer heard Mark come home late, drunk as usual. She was usually asleep, but this night she had a very bad headache and could not sleep. She tossed and turned, and as she heard the front door shut, she heard Grace's door open. She figured he was saying goodnight. She waited for him to come out, but he didn't.

She quietly got up and went to Grace's door and opened it as quietly as she could. She was shocked! Mark was passed out, Grace was sobbing, and tears were running down her little face. She was trying her hardest to cry quietly, as her dad had passed out across her with his hand where it should not be.

Jennifer screamed at Mark, "Get out! Get out of here now! Move it, and do not come back, or I will call the cops!"

He was too drunk to fight for a change, and he got into his truck and sped off down the road. The next day, Jennifer took Grace to the police. She hated to put her little girl through the ordeal she was about to go through, but she loved her daughter. After Grace was examined, Mark was arrested for child molestation. He had tried to talk to Jennifer. He made excuses and tried to tell her that she did not see what she thought she saw, but Jennifer knew better.

The exam the police had done on Grace at the hospital nearby proved that Mark had been molesting his own daughter. What was even worse was that the exam proved it was not the first time. He was charged with a first-degree felony, criminal sexual conduct with a minor.

******

The court day had come, and Mark was being tried at the Lexington County Courthouse. Jennifer was full of emotions and was angry at Mark for doing this to their little girl. She was angry at him for ruining their marriage and angry and scared at the fact that she had no job and now had to take care of her little girls all by herself.

Robert Miller, or Bobby as people called him, was the assistant DA and had a special dislike for these kinds of cases. He had just been promoted to this office, and his wife had just found out she was pregnant. They had only been married a couple of years, but he could not fathom doing anything like this, and it angered him. He was handling the case and was determined to make sure Mark was put away for a long time.

During the trial, Robert looked over at Jennifer and Grace, and his heart went out to them—such a sweet, innocent little face and beautiful long, curly, brunette hair. Robert could not understand how this could happen and was determined to do his best to make Mark pay for his actions. Mark was sentenced to twenty-five years in prison, to be served day to day.

After the verdict, Jennifer filed for divorce and got a job at the nearby Walmart. Things happened so fast that Jennifer hardly had time to process everything. She had to find a cheaper place to live and find a friend to babysit the girls and she needed to make enough to support them.

******

Sistercare is a program of services for battered women and their children residing in Fairfield, Kershaw, Lexington, Newberry, and Richland Counties in South Carolina. They helped Jennifer to apply for assistance. She was approved, and she received financial assistance. It helped a lot, but she hated having to rely on others for help.

One day, during a three-day weekend that she happened to get off, the realization of it all came crashing down on her, and Jennifer began to sob profusely! She did not realize that she had blamed her precious little girl for the loss of her marriage, Jennifer lost control. Later, Grace came into Jennifer's room to ask her what she was doing and to tell her that she needed her help with Jolisa, who was two now.

"Mommy, Mommy, Jolisa is getting into the refrigerator. She is pulling things out and making a mess! Mommy," Grace yelled.

"Go away, Grace. I need to be alone!" Jennifer yelled back at her.

Grace replied, "But, Mommy, Jolisa!"

At that moment the overwhelming emotion of everything that had happened seemed to cave in all at once. Jennifer grabbed Grace's arm and squeezed tight, bruising it; and she slapped her across the face.

"Stop it, stop it, and leave me alone! It is your fault! Your dad is gone because of you!"

She slapped Grace again and again, not realizing what she was doing. The anger of it all; of who Mark had become since moving to Columbia, the loss of her marriage, and seeing what he had done to their daughter, came crashing down, and Jennifer lost it. She exploded, and Grace was in the wrong place at the wrong time. At the last slap, Grace fell to the floor, crying and crying. She lay there, face whelped and arms bruised. She pulled herself up and ran to her room and cried.

She heard Jolisa crying. She knew she had to have seen what happened to her and she didn't want her mommy to do the same thing to Jolisa. She gathered Jolisa up and put her in her crib for a nap and went into her room and cried herself to sleep.

Grace woke up late that afternoon and was scared to move, scared to do anything, and thought to herself, did I make Daddy do those things? Did I make Daddy leave? What is wrong with me?

Jennifer kept Grace home from school until the bruising went away and tried to apologize, but the damage was done. Once again, the happy little girl Grace had once been, seemed to be gone forever. Grace was quiet and subdued.

When she went back to school, even her teachers knew something was wrong. Grace seemed to be afraid of people when before the change, she had been very happy and outgoing. They knew about the ordeal with her father because Jennifer had told them, but they did not know what else was going on at home now.

Jennifer knew it was not her little girl's fault, but she could not help herself. The anger she could not let go of seemed to always come out at Grace. This went on for a couple of years until Jennifer met someone else and married again. The anger she had felt was gone, but the damage to Grace had already been done. It had created in her tremendous insecurity and low self-esteem, not to mention deep-seated fear. Her relationship with her mom was never the same. They lived in the same house but were almost strangers. Jennifer had tried to make amends, she loved her daughter, but Grace could not move past the abuse.

******

The years had passed, and Grace was in high school now, she felt worthless and was quiet and kept to herself. Grace had a few friends, but most of the time, she liked being alone. She seemed to walk around in a state of depression. Even though she had a few friends, it did not change the way she felt inside. The happy little girl she used to be with a family that loved her, seemed as if it was someone else's life. The happy memories she once knew had faded away.

All Grace knew now, was the feeling of not being wanted or loved. Grace felt all alone and knew something was wrong deep inside, but did not know why. She was fourteen years old now, and the abuse she had suffered as a child with her dad and later her mom, had been buried deep within her heart. The memory of it was too painful for her to let surface, so she buried it so deep she could barely even remember the events that took place. All she could remember was her dad did something wrong and was sent to jail. When someone tried to ask her about her father, she refused to talk about him. Nevertheless, there was a pain that was rooted deep within her heart, and it resonated throughout her whole spirit.

One day, it became too much to deal with, and Grace had decided to end it all. She felt as if no one loved her, and the pain in her heart was just too much to bear any longer. Her dad had hurt her and was gone. Her mom hurt her, and pain and hurt was what she came to believe about everyone. She believed that everyone wanted to hurt her or to leave her.

Grace went to the store and bought three boxes of over-the-counter sleeping pills and decided to end it all. She locked herself in the bathroom and took every one of the pills. The only ones home were Grace and her younger sister.

Jolisa stood outside the bathroom door, pounding on it, "Grace, open up. You have been in there long enough, and I really have to go! Open up!"

Jolisa stood there, pounding and yelling; and right about that time, their mother came home early from work. She had a very bad headache and had left work early. She heard the commotion and asked, "What is going on? I can hear you all the way outside?"

"Mom," Jolisa replied, "Grace has been in there for almost half an hour, and I really have to go."

Jennifer came up to the door and yelled out to Grace, "Grace, open this door up right now!"

When after a couple of times of commanding her to open the door and no answer, she knew something was wrong. She gained a strength she did not know she had and kicked the door open. She could not believe what she saw. There was Grace on the floor, passed out, with the boxes of sleeping pills on the floor beside her.

"Grace!" Jennifer screamed, "Grace! Jolisa, call 911!"

Jennifer grabbed one of the boxes and stuffed them into her pocket. She cradled her daughter as they waited for the ambulance to arrive.

They began working on her as soon as they arrived and Grace was taken to Lexington Medical Center, which was a short drive away. They pumped her stomach, and Grace lay there, unconscious.

Jennifer sat beside her little girl's bed and cried, "Oh dear God, I know you and I have not been on good terms for some time now, but please save my little girl."

She sat beside Grace and laid her head across Grace's body. She cried and cried. It had been two days when Grace finally woke up. Jennifer and Jolisa were so relieved.

Because she tried to commit suicide, Grace had to visit a psychologist. She went to the appointments, but she only went through the motions. She did not know where the pain was coming from concerning her dad. She had suppressed the pain and didn't even remember it, so she had nothing to tell them.

She just told them what she knew. She told them about the abuse she suffered as a child, at the hands of her mom. She told them that she and her mom were good right now and that she didn't abuse her any longer. She just knew she was hurting and did not know why.

She continued to go through the motions. She just pretended to listen and understand, as they talked to her. She had become very good at that and told them what she knew they wanted to hear. Apparently, she was believable enough, so they released her.

After the suicide attempt, her mom tried extra hard to show Grace just how much she loved her. But the pain that was rooted in Grace's heart ran too deep. It wasn't even her mom that she felt was the cause of her pain, but it was from something she could not remember. Something she had seemed to block out. Every act of love from anyone, just sank into Grace's mind because it was impossible to believe that anyone could love her.

******

It has been an hour since Grace began her morning walk along the beach, lost in her memories. She looked up and thought, Thank you, God, that you have healed my heart so well, that I can think back, and the heartache is no longer there.

Thank you, Father, for being the Father that mine could not be.

2

The Teenage Years

It was Saturday, and Grace had been up for hours. She loved to get up before the sun came up, so she could sit on her porch, drink her coffee, and watch the sunrise.

Grace had become a photographer since receiving Jesus. The light of God's love seemed to have awakened something within her and she could see things in a whole new light. It showed in her pictures. She made quite a good living at it. She loved to paint as well, but only as a hobby. Although she was a very good and accomplished painter, she liked to paint for relaxation, more than for a living.

As she sat and drank her coffee, she took a paintbrush in hand and worked on a new painting of the sunrise. Painting the sun rising over the water was her favorite thing to paint. She felt more alive when she was painting or taking pictures than at any other time. She enjoyed bringing life to the canvas of what she was painting or the pictures she was taking. Finishing up her coffee, she got up and changed her clothes to take her morning walk.

As she started down the beach, she waved to Mr. Henry, an older man who had lived on the beach with his wife, for most of their life. They used to take morning walks also, along with Sissy, their golden retriever that seemed to adopt them three years ago. His wife, Bonnie, passed away last year; and Mr. Henry continued his morning walks alone, except for Sissy.

He once said, "I feel so close to Bonnie when I walk out here. It is as if she is right beside me." He always had a smile and would wave as Grace walked by. Sometimes, they even walked down the beach together. Today was no exception.

"Paint anything new lately?" Mr. Henry asked.

"I've started another sunrise. This time, I am adding a little more pinks in the sky and a touch of white froth upon the waves, as they splash their way into the coast," Grace replied.

"Sounds beautiful. You will have to let me see it when you are done!" Mr. Henry said as Grace walked past.

"Sure, this one is just for fun, so if you like it, you can have it!"

And with that, they waved each other on. She was still lost in her thoughts, so she did not stay to talk. She did not understand why the past had been on her mind so much lately, but here it was again. The sun was up now and still just as beautiful, and it was a little cooler than yesterday. But at least the sun was out, she thought.

******

Her mind drifted back to a time when she was in high School. Although Grace was a beautiful girl, she never saw herself that way, and with the memories of the abuse she had suffered buried deep inside, she didn't understand why. She had a few girlfriends but did not associate with the "in crowd" of girls. She never felt worthy, nor did she feel as if she could attract the attention of any boys who hung with that crowd. So the boyfriends she dated, which were not very many, only used her for one thing; and it was not her heart.

The one thing that she did not falter on was her schoolwork. Grace liked school and learning very much, and how she felt about herself never got in the way of her love for learning, so she did very well in school.

Grace's emotions ran rampant. She was always either depressed, full of anxiety, or angry. Although Grace never tried to commit suicide again, she did not want to live anymore. The after-effects from the failed attempt were not something she wanted to go through again. Her emotions were uncontrollable, and she did not know why. School was the only thing she could control, and that was why she liked it so much.

Grace felt ashamed of herself, as though all the bad stuff that had happened in the past was her fault. She developed an eating disorder and saw herself as ugly, so she would force herself to throw up, and it was beginning to show.

Bobby was a boy she had dated for the last couple of years in high school. He was a "bad boy," so to speak, and when he received his driver's license in his senior year, it was bad news for Grace. On the weekends, they used to go out; and Grace, who had been drinking before to numb the pain in her heart, started drinking even more, along with Bobby. She didn't think anyone who wanted anything out of life as far as a future would want her, so in her misplaced perception, she stayed with Bobby. He would drink a little too much and get rough with her. She put up with it thinking, as before, that she deserved it.

Grace felt ashamed of herself most of the time and felt as if her emotional and family problems were all her fault. Grace had been so abused and her spirit so broken, she learned not to expect anything else and was afraid of everyone, especially Bobby.

Bobby grew more and more controlling and abusive, and it got so bad, that he forbade her to have anything to do with her friends. He overheard them one day telling her that, as pretty as she was, she could get a guy who would respect her more than he does. With that, upon his command, her friendship with them ended, and now the only one in her life was Bobby, and that was just the way he wanted it. According to him, she was his property and would do as he wanted and even think what he wanted her to think.

Grace didn't realize that is exactly what Satan wants of us—to be enslaved, oppressed, and depressed—with no life in our spirits.

"They promise them freedom, while they themselves are slaves of depravity—for 'people are slaves to whatever has mastered them'" 2 Peter 2:19.

Grace went through the rest of high school in a daze, like an obedient robot that did not know any better. She was ordered by Bobby to wait at the front entrance for him and not to move or talk to anyone. One day, a new boy saw her standing there and started making friendly conversation. He was waiting for some friends as well. It was innocent and passing-the-time sort of conversation, but as soon as Bobby walked up and saw Grace talking to him, he flew into a jealous rage!

He yelled, "Grace, come on! I told you not to talk to anyone! Come on, now!"

Everyone was looking, due to the loud rage in his voice. Grace felt completely humiliated and, as usual, felt as if it was her fault. She had not obeyed. That day, he didn't even take her home. He stopped at the store, bought some beer, and drove up to his family's cabin at the lake. At first, she thought his anger had subsided, but not so. After about six beers, reeking of alcohol, he laid into her.

"I told you not to talk to anyone! Are you that stupid that you cannot follow instructions? You belong to me, and you are not allowed to talk to anyone unless I say it is okay. Do you understand?"

And with that, he slapped her across the face again and again, and even asked, "Whose fault is it that you are being beaten right now? Whose?"

With tears running down her face, she sheepishly said, "Mine."

"What are you going to do about it?" Bobby asked, motioning downward.

Like an obedient slave, she got down on her knees and begged for forgiveness and said, "I am sorry, and I will not talk to anyone unless you say it is okay."

He grabbed her by the hair and said, "You belong to me, you are my property, and what you do and who you talk to must be okay with me first!"

Wiping the tears from her face, she said, "Okay, I promise."

Acting as if nothing had happened and smelling of sour beer and spilling the beer all over her as if on purpose, he took her over and over. They did not leave the cabin all weekend. After that, if she had any respect for herself at all, it was gone now. Grace felt dirty and about as low as anyone could feel, short of being dead.

Grace did graduate high school, and believe it or not, so did Bobby. He got a job at a local construction company, and as much as Grace wanted to go to college, Bobby would not allow it. He knew she would gain too much knowledge and independence and would want to leave him.

A short time later, they married and got an apartment together, and he allowed her to get a job at a nearby café, and, of course, he controlled all the money. She had to give it all, tips and wages over to Bobby.

It wasn't long before he made her quit that job; he did not like the guys making passes at her, so she took another one at a nearby hobby store. She liked it. The hours were great, with no late nights, and she loved looking at everything in the paint section. She had never tried to paint but thought, *Someday, I would like to try my hand at painting.*

Bobby continued his controlling ways, and things got even worse, now that they were married. He would go out with the guys and come home reeking of alcohol and cheap perfume. She knew he was seeing someone else and tried to confront him one night.

"I know you have been with someone else. We are married, and that means you, as well as me," she boldly said for the first time. In fact, she shouted at him. He looked at her as if she had just committed a serious crime.

He whirled around and, with a look of rage in his eyes, slapped her so hard she almost flew across the room and yelled, "What did you just say? What did you say?" He said it again and again, grabbing her up by the hair.

"I'm sorry. I'm sorry!" Grace cried.

"You better be. Don't you ever question me again! I am the man of the house. I own you, and don't you forget it. What I do or don't is none of your business! All that matters is I come home to you, right?"

Wiping the tears from her eyes and face all whelped and red, Grace could hardly utter the words, "Right, I'm sorry, and I won't do it again."

Grace never questioned him again. Grace felt even worse than ever and wondered why she had even been born. That feeling seemed to grasp her heart to the very core of it, and people at work even noticed and questioned her. They could see the already subdued Grace was even more so now. Grace had completely walled herself in from everyone and was terribly afraid to let anyone in because, as she thought, everyone just wanted to use me or hurt me. Her depression was trying to consume her. When questioned, she would say, "It's nothing," and go about her work. She was extremely afraid for anyone to find out about her life.

******

A few weeks went by, and a new girl named Lily seemed to take notice of Grace. They quickly became friends, which was odd for Grace to let anyone in. But, somehow Grace felt comfortable around her and was drawn to her. It felt as if she had known her all her life.

This took everyone at the store by surprise, because Grace never really talked to anyone. Grace still kept her abusive home life a secret, but felt as if she could tell Lily anything, even if she dared.

Grace was unaware that Lily was a Christian, and the gentleness Lily had was due to her faith in Christ. Lily knew that there was something off about Grace—sort of rigid. Not in a prideful, stuffy way, but in a fearful way, as if she was consumed in it. Maybe that is why she felt drawn to her and sensed that God had brought them together. But, she did not know why yet. She kept Grace in her daily prayers and knew that God would reveal it, or that Grace would open up when the time was right. She did not push it.

******

Bobby grew more and more sure of himself and began to go away for the weekend periodically. Grace knew where he was, but did not dare say anything. He would come home from his escapades smelling of perfume and beer and kiss her on the cheek, as if he had been on a business trip. As the weeks went by, Bobby grew more and more abusive. The slightest little thing Grace would say, or even if she did not have dinner set and on the table when he did decide to come home, he would fly off into one of his rages. Grace would end up on the floor from the other end of his fists. Grace became robotic at home, going through the motions of life and not expecting anything different. Bobby, so sure of his control over Grace now, came home one evening and asked Grace,

"I need you to buy some perfume for me to give Pamela, a girl I know." He glared at her, as he spoke up again. "You get paid tomorrow, right?"

"Yes," she said.

"Well, use some of that," he said, glaring at her again and daring her to say anything.

Grace replied as if she was a little girl about to get into trouble with her daddy, "Of course." Sure enough, Grace obeyed.

Time went by, and the abuse decreased, mainly because Bobby was gone a lot; but even though he was gone, he expected Grace to stay at home, alone. He would even call to make sure she was there. Grace wasn't even allowed to call her sister, Jolisa. He feared that Jolisa would talk her into leaving him. He was not treating Grace with respect, or even like another human being, but he did not want her to leave and expected her to be there when he decided he needed her.

The friendship between Lily and Grace grew; and at

work, as much as possible, they were together on every break. Lily got bold one day on their lunch break and asked Grace, "You know I love you like a sister and would never do anything to hurt you, right? I would never tell anything that you tell me in secret to anyone?"

Grace looked at Lily with a look of confusion. She did not know what she was getting at and replied, "I guess so. Why do you ask?"

"Well, since we have met, I have noticed the way you look when anyone pays you a compliment. You kind of bury your face, as if you don't believe it. Don't you know how beautiful you are? Who hurt you? Who did this to you? Who has made you feel so worthless? I don't mean to pry, but that is the impression I get by your demeanor, and I do not like it! You have a precious and sweet spirit, and you are beautiful! Don't you know that?" Lily said with a smile on her face. She hugged Grace in a way that screamed sincere love.

Grace did not know what to do with that, but she welcomed Lily's friendly embrace and began to cry and sob. "I'm sorry, Lily. I don't mean to cry, but no one has told me that in many years, not since I was a little girl, but I cannot talk about it."

Lily looked back at her and said, "Whenever you are ready, I'm here."

They nodded at each other and went back to work. During the rest of Grace's shift, she pondered over the words Lily spoke. They made her feel good, and it was a feeling she had not experienced in quite some time.

******

Bobby came home from work one Friday with a smug look on his face. He was so sure of his hold over Grace and arrogantly told her, "I am going away for a week, and I expect you to be here when I get back. Make sure my clothes are washed for work."

Grace did not know what came over her, but before she knew what she was saying, she yelled at him, "I know where you are going, who you are going with, and, no, you are not going, and, no, you will not go away with Pamela, and, no, I will not wash your clothes, and, no, you will not see her anymore!"

A look of complete shock filled Bobby's face; he could not believe what he was hearing! She had never dared talk to him like that, and he flew into another one of his rages. He slapped her and slapped her and poured the beer he was drinking on the floor and shoved her face into it and told her to clean it up! He told her that the job she was working at was putting ideas in her head, and she was ordered to quit.

"Who is the boss of this household? I am, and who owns you? Me! I will do what I want and when I want and with whoever I want! Don't forget it! Now what do you have to say?"

Grace was so bruised, and her arm hurt so badly from the way he had grabbed her that she could hardly move or speak.

In a meek voice, Grace looked up at him and said, "You are the boss, and I belong to you."

As if nothing was wrong, Bobby packed his bags and told her he would be home in a week.

Something came over her. Grace suddenly remembered the words Lily had said, *"You are precious."*

Little did she know then that it was the Holy Spirit bringing those words to remembrance. God does not like the ones he created out of love to live lives of abuse and captivity.

"I will weep in secret because of your pride; my eyes will weep bitterly, overflowing with tears, because the Lord's flock will be taken captive" Jeremiah 13:17.

As soon as he left, Grace got up, as if someone else was controlling her and called Lily. Grace did not say why but said she needed her right away. Lily could tell it was serious and came rushing over.

The moment Lily walked in, she knew what was happening. Lily knew Grace was being abused and severely. Lily held her and listened as Grace told her about her life with Bobby, high school, and everything. She told her how controlling he was and how she could not even call her sister, go to college, or even have friends. She told her about Bobby's affairs and where he was now and how this particular fight started. Lily looked at her with pride in her eyes.

"I am so sorry that he has been hurting you. He has no right. He is just another human being, just like you. Being your husband does not give him the right to beat you and take advantage of you! However, with that said, I am so proud of you that you stood up for yourself. You are too young and too beautiful inside and out to be treated like that! You are coming home with me, and I will not take no for an answer. This is the last day you suffer at his hands. She packed her bags and threw her belongings, pictures, and clothes in a box.

It was late when they were done, but Lily did not want Grace to come back for anything. She left everything else, and with Lily's help, they got all her belongings and put them in the back of Lily's Jeep Cherokee, and the next stop was the police station.

Lily explained that he would come after her, and she needed the police to have pictures of her bruises. Grace filed the reports, and then the police sent her to the hospital for further examination. They discovered through the tests they ran that she had been beaten before this, and the doctors noted this in their report to the police.

The police told her that a restraining order is legal and he could go to jail if he came near her or tried to hurt her again. They also said they could not watch Bobby's every move and warned her to take precautions and that keeping the restraint was up to her. They could only do so much but could not help her if she decided to go back to him.

They also directed her to Sistercare, a wonderful organization for battered women, which helped her to get started in filing the paperwork for a restraining order, an order of protection with the Family Court of the West Columbia Municipal Courthouse. Grace knew she faced a battle in the days ahead, but she had a strength that she never she had before and did not know exactly where it came from. She was beginning to like it very much.

Lily called in to work for Grace, and with her permission, she told their boss everything that was going on with Grace and her abusive husband. Brent was all too happy to be able to help her and told her to take all the time she needed.

The hearing was set. Her friends from work came to testify, and the pictures the police had taken were brought forth for evidence, and the order of protection was issued. Brent, Grace's boss, had given her enough time off to take care of all this. His heart went out to her when he saw how bruised and beaten she was and knew she needed the time. She did not know where Lily came from, or even understand why the two grew to be such good friends in such a short time, but Lily had become a cherished friend. She was like a sister, like Jolisa, the one she hardly knew and yet missed dearly. A battle was nearing and after the events of the past few days.

That evening, Grace finally settled in and quickly fell asleep, as soon as her head hit the pillow.

In the next room, Lily was on her knees praying, "Lord, protect her and keep her safe. Guide her and be her advocate. Show her what true love looks like and what love is and, most of all, show her who you are to her. In Jesus's name, amen."

Lily got up off her knees and could hear in her heart, that *this battle belongs to the Lord. It is mine, and I will watch over her coming and her going both now and forevermore.*

Lily looked up and smiled and said, "That is why I love you so much. Your love, your salvation and protection, and your loving eyes are always watching over us. Thank you, Father."

3

The Battle to Freedom

Grace had to drive up to the mountains in the coming week to take some pictures of the mountain scenery for a travel magazine. Fall was a wonderful time to take pictures of the mountains. She did not mind the drive. She loved the mountains almost as much as she loved the beach. Grace asked Mr. Henry to keep an eye on her house while she was away. He didn't mind it a bit. It made him feel useful and needed.

Grace was traveling to Cherokee, North Carolina, and up into the Blue Ridge Parkway. The parkway would be a great place to take pictures. The trees that covered the parkway had started to change their colors. It was as if an artist took a paintbrush to them. The colors were a beautiful blend of orange, deep red, yellow, and green. Grace loved driving along the Blue Ridge Parkway this time of year. The view was awe-inspiring, and at the sight of it all, she wondered, how can anyone see the beauty of the mountains and array of colors and not believe in God?

It was about a five-hour drive, and she would be gone for five days. Although she was up for it, she was not up for the way her mind seemed to drift back to the past lately.

******

About an hour into her driving, sure enough, the memories came flooding back. She remembered the peace she felt waking up in Lily's home. It was a feeling she was not used to at all, and she knew there was a storm waiting to catch up to her as soon as Bobby came home and found the restraining order taped to the door.

Lily and Grace were truly blessed to work at a place that was like a little home. Lily called Brent again to keep him up-to-date on everything, and he said, "Bring it on! If he comes here and makes trouble, I will call the police. Don't worry, and tell Grace to take whatever time she needs."

Lily told Grace what their boss had said, and she just broke down in tears. "I can't believe how great you all are being to me. I don't know what I would do without you. Thank you so much."

Lily turned to her and smiled. "That is what family does."

They moved Grace's car into Lily's garage to conceal it from Bobby searching for Grace. They were both grateful that Grace had never mentioned Lily or their friendship.

As expected, Bobby called Saturday evening before he was to return home, expecting Grace to be home waiting for him like a dutiful wife while he was away on his affair. The arrogance!

No answer. He called again and the same, no answer. This infuriated him, thinking, she should be up and waiting for his call! He reasoned to himself that she was asleep. He never imagined she would dare leave him. Sunday afternoon, Bobby drove up to the house, expecting

Grace to be inside fixing his dinner, with his clothes all washed. In all his conceit, he did not expect that not only were his clothes not washed and all over the floor, but Grace would be gone and nowhere to be found!

He turned the key and opened the door and thought it strange to be so quiet. *Still calm*, he thought, *she must be out back*. He called out to her and called again, walking angrily now out to the back, and she was not there either! He yelled even more loudly now, "Grace, where are you? Come out now, or I am going to beat you good!" There was a look of pure fury in his eyes. You could almost see the fire in them; he was so angry. He searched all over, throwing things and yelling. It was as if a monster, even more so than the one that existed before, had been unleashed! He was so angry about Grace not being home, that he did not even notice the restraining order taped to the door.

He got into his car and drove to the store, it was all dark and closed up. He drove all over. Grace was nowhere to be found.

He drove to her mom's house and came up pounding on the door. "Where is Grace? Where is she? I know she is in there!"

Sam, Jennifer's new husband, opened the door, and before he could say or do anything, Bobby rushed into the house looking all over. "Where is she? Where is Grace?"

Sam, angry at the outburst that disrupted his Sunday, said, "Grace is not here, and we have not heard from her or seen her since you two got married! By the way you are acting, I wouldn't tell you even if I knew. Now get out of my house before I call the police!"

Sam was a very big man and stood his ground. He was tall and very muscular and grabbed Bobby and threw him outside, saying again, "You darken my door again, and in that tone, it will be your last time!"

Like a whipped puppy, Bobby got into his car and sped off down the road. That was a sight that no one had ever seen before in him.

Sam looked over at Jennifer and said, "I don't know what is going on, but it seems as if Grace has come to her senses and left him. We had better call the police and report this, so it is on record, in case he finds Grace and tries to do something."

Jennifer was worried, and she warned Jolisa, who was just entering her senior year of high school. Jennifer had changed a lot since she had married Sam. Sam was a Christian and eventually, after they had begun dating, he inspired Jennifer to come to church. Both Jennifer and Jolisa started going, and it was not long afterward that they were both saved. They had both tried to get in touch with Grace but to no avail. Jennifer longed to see her daughter. She missed her terribly and had repented to the Lord for her actions and made peace with Jolisa. She longed to make peace with Grace and have her back in her life again. Now, with this new event, she was very worried about her. That night they sat together, Sam, Jennifer, and Jolisa, and prayed for Grace.

On the other side of town, in Lily's house, Lily was doing the same thing, kneeling beside her bed. She was also praying for Grace.

Bobby was even angrier now, even more so by the way Sam had treated him. It did not matter how well deserved, but his arrogance would not allow him to believe that he was at any fault in any of it. In his mind, this was all Grace's fault. She should have been home waiting to wait on him hand and foot and welcome him with a smile on her face. He could not believe the audacity of her actually leaving him! He was furious and could hardly sleep.

The next day, he called in sick and went to the hobby store where Grace worked. By the expression on his face, the manager knew who he was and informed the girl at the customer service desk to call the police if he started to get out of hand. Bobby went straight over to the manager and, in a very loud voice, yelled, "Where is Grace? Where is my wife? Where are you all hiding her?"

Brent, the manager, tried to keep it as low-key as it was in his means to do. He replied, "I am not sure where she is. Grace called in sick Saturday and today as well. We have not heard from her. Can I tell her you are looking for her if she calls? I assumed if she was sick that she would be at home?"

Fury was coming out of Bobby's eyes. He shouted back at him, "I don't believe that you do not know where she is, but in any case, if I find out you are lying, I will be back. I will destroy you and everything in this store!"

With that, he knocked over a few shelves that displayed merchandise, damaging some of it, as if to show how powerful he was, and stormed out the door. Sherry, who was standing nearby, did not know what was going on with Grace. By the way her husband was acting, she assumed that Grace would be in severe trouble if Bobby found her and decided to record everything on her phone. It was a good thing because later they would need that recording.

After he had left, Brent called Lily and told her that Bobby was just there and what state he was in and to keep Grace there for another week. He said he would give her a week's vacation pay. Lily took Grace to see her brother, who was an attorney, to help Grace file for divorce. Due to everything Grace had been through and the fact that she was a friend of his sister's, Thomas took the case for free.

Grace was amazed at the support she was receiving. Bobby had kept her so isolated she had forgotten what having friends was like. The last friends she had were in high school, and that seemed like such a long time ago.

When he returned home, Bobby finally saw the restraining orders taped to his door, and he exploded! He was so angry he could not control himself and drove by the hobby store every day during the next week. By this time, every shift was made aware of him and was ready to call the police.

One time, Sherry, who was on duty again, called the police as soon as she saw him get out of his car. He stormed in and didn't even stop to talk, but ranted and raved around the store, calling out for Grace.

"Grace, I know you are here! Come out right now! Stop hiding! You don't come out right now, I swear I'm going to kill you the moment I get my hands on you!"

Still, he found no Grace, and by this time, the police showed up and hauled him off to jail. They kept him overnight and released him the next day, warning him to stay away, but that only infuriated him more.

The week of vacation was up, and Grace knew she could not hide any longer and she had to go back to work. Grace and Lily took separate cars, so if Bobby was watching he would not know that she was staying with her. Bobby was driving by the store every day, and they had warned Grace and told her to be careful. Sure enough, late that afternoon, right about the time Grace was about to get off, in came Bobby. He spotted her right away.

"Where have you been hiding, and what is the meaning of this restraining order? Do you really think you can keep me away from you? You are mine, and you need to get back home now!"

Grace tried to stay away from his grasp, moving from aisle to aisle, and Sherry recorded the whole thing again while the manager called the police and then calmly tried to make him leave.

Bobby spun around to confront Brent. "Who do you think you are to tell me to leave and to leave my wife alone? I will beat you senseless."

Brent, once again in a calm voice, said, "Bobby, we don't want any trouble. Grace does not want to go with you, so please just go home before things get worse."

Bobby was shouting as loud as he could and not caring.

"I will do what I please, and just who are you to tell me what my wife wants? I make the decisions for her! Grace, come now!"

Grace fearfully looked at him and, in a timid voice, said, "Bobby, it is over. I will not be beaten by you anymore, and I am filing for divorce."

The rage he felt right then was more than he could handle, and somehow he made it to where Grace was and grabbed her. She fell to the floor, and he began dragging her by the hair. He stopped along the way, and he took his fist and swung it right across her face. He yelled at her,

"You are mine, and I will do what I please. You are not filing for divorce, even if I have to keep you chained up. And what do you mean by filing a restraining order against me? Did you think that piece of paper or anyone else could keep me away from you? Now come on! We are going home."

Bobby looked at everyone, daring them to make a move while he kept dragging Grace with her swollen and bloody face across the floor.

Just in time, right before he reached the door, the police came barreling in with guns raised and shouted,

"Put her down now, or we will shoot!"

He tried to maneuver around them, but could not, and everyone was amazed at how quickly he dropped Grace after that. They expected him to put up more of a fight. They carted him off to jail, and he would probably be there a while from the damage to the store, breaking the restraining order, and not to mention the abuse to Grace. They called an ambulance, and as they were about to wheel Grace away, everyone in the store came over to her.

Knowing she would feel humiliated, they said, almost in unison, "Grace, we are proud of you. So many women do not stand up to their abusers, but you left, and you stood up to him, and for that, we applaud you."

Grace, as painful as it was, began to cry and said, "Thank you so much. I don't know what I would do without you."

Brent was the last one to tell her goodbye and bent down and whispered, "Don't worry about your job either. This was not your fault, and it will be here when you recover. Take all the time you need." He squeezed her hand in a comforting way and then waved to Grace and Lily, who were accompanying her to the hospital.

Grace was in the hospital for a while. She had an orbital fracture, which is a break in one of the bones that make up the orbit. Since the orbit is the seat of the globe (the eye), an orbital fracture can be a serious and sight-threatening break. The orbit is made up of parts of six bones: the frontal, ethmoidal, lacrimal, sphenoid, maxilla, and zygomatic. A break in the orbit portion of one or more of these six bones is an orbital fracture (Web MD). It would take even longer for her to recover emotionally from the trauma she endured.

Sherry and Lily took the recorded videos from Sherry's phone to the police. They had plenty of evidence and witnesses to file charges. Bobby was brought up on charges for the damages done in the store and the disturbance. He was charged with public disorderly conduct and malicious injury to personal property and with violating the restraining order. His bond was denied based on the evidence presented. He was sentenced to ninety days in jail, by the city of West Columbia Municipal Court.

It just so happened that the same prosecutor, who was much older now, was the one who prosecuted her dad for sexual abuse. He was overseeing the trial of Bobby for the assault on Grace. He remembered Grace, and his heart went out to her. First, she had to overcome the abuse by her dad, and now the abuse by her husband. It broke his heart, and he was going for the fullest sentence he could get for Bobby.

A few weeks went by and Bobby's court date finally came. His case went to general sessions in the Lexington County Courthouse. Robert Miller, the prosecutor, was sure that he had enough evidence to put Bobby away for a while. The store manager Brent and Shirley, along with

Lily, all testified on Grace's behalf. The pictures and videos from the store incident, along with the pictures from the police and doctors' reports from the previous attack, were all presented during the trial. Robert was pleased with the outcome. Bobby was charged with criminal domestic violence with a high-and-aggravated-nature felony and received ten years and all charges to be served consecutive day to day. He also had to take part in counseling and an anger management class.

Grace was relieved and hoped that the counseling that he would have to go through as a part of his sentence would get to the bottom of his problem. She hoped he would learn why he was so abusive, because she did not want him to come after her again when and if he ever got released from jail.

This wasn't over by a long shot. Grace had a lot of emotional scars within that needed to be healed, and now that she was in a place away from Bobby, the healing process could begin.

The Lord builds up Jerusalem; he gathers the outcasts of Israel. He heals the brokenhearted and binds up their wounds.
—Psalm 147:2–3

4

∞

A New Beginning

It was a beautiful day! The sun was shining, and the air was cool and brisk. You could feel winter trying to push its way through. The mountains were breathtaking. Grace had a wonderful mountain view from her hotel bedroom. She opened the windows and sat there with her morning coffee and just drank in the mountain scenery.

Today she decided she would drive through the back roads of Cherokee. They had lots of fruit stands along the highway of people selling apples. They were plentiful in this part of the country, and she wanted to buy some for her and Mr. Henry. Besides that, the Cherokee Indian Village would prove to be a successful venture in taking pictures for the magazine. It had plenty of old mountain farms and abandoned old houses left over from years and years ago to photograph. They make great pictures in the right setting. Along the roadside, there were also rivers that flowed down from the mountains, with people sitting alongside, fishing. She would have a lot of pictures to bring back!

Tomorrow, she planned to drive up the Blue Ridge Parkway, and there would be just as many magnificent shots there. There were trails and overlooks that had grand views, hundreds of feet down the mountainside. Grace had decided if she ever moved again that this would be the place. There was much more to do and see in the mountains than on the beach,

35

but somehow the beach with the ocean waters never-ending, instilled in her the calmness she needed after everything that happened with Bobby.

It was time to go. Camera equipment and jacket in hand, Grace was off. She loved this drive. It was so peaceful, and as she drank in the beauty of the mountains, her mind drifted back in time once again.

******

After the trial was over and she was sure that Bobby would be in jail for a while, Grace decided to change her name. Her married name was Grace Robertson, and her maiden name was Williams, but she decided to change it to Thompson—something totally different—so when and if Bobby ever got out he could not find her.

It had been almost a week since Bobby was sentenced. It was Friday, and by chance, Lily was off on Saturday. Lily decided that after everything that happened Grace needed to do something fun. She told Grace that they were going to the beach for the weekend, so they packed up and headed for Myrtle Beach.

They managed to find a hotel with a room overlooking the beach, and Grace felt a calmness sweep over her as they sat on their balcony and looked out at the ocean with the waves rolling onto the shore. They sat there and watched the people having fun and talked and talked. Grace almost forgot the life of misery she came from and felt a sense of relief. Internally, she was still a complete mess.

Grace was twenty-three years old and had been controlled by Bobby for seven years. That was all she knew and she would have to learn about being independent; besides that, it was okay to be who she was and to have likes and dislikes of her own. She was made to feel as if she wasn't human or allowed to have feelings of her own or even make a decision on her own. She had to learn to live; and not only that, there was the low self-esteem, depression, the feeling of worthlessness, and shame that needed to be weeded out of her heart and mind. The walls needed to come down. She had to learn that she did not deserve what happened and it was not normal or her fault. It was the beginning of a new life for her, but there would still be a long road ahead.

They were having a wonderful time. They went out to a seafood restaurant and then walked on the beach. It was a new feeling for Grace to go somewhere and not have to worry about what she said or did or whom she talked to for fear of making Bobby angry.

Lily could still see the rigid fear screaming from within Grace by her actions, and she prayed silently for the Lord to walk her through each step of her new life and to show her that it was going to be all right. That fearful feeling was still there in the background of her heart. With every step, every new adventure taken on her own, no matter how great or small, it was as if she was walking a tightrope. She felt that with one wrong move, she would fall.

As the evening went on, Lily could tell that Grace was becoming more and more relaxed. As they walked on the beach, they laughed and were having a good time. This was a side of Grace that Lily had not seen, and she silently prayed, *Thank you, God*. They stopped and sat on the beach when they reached their hotel and looked out at the ocean and watched the waves roll in. It was so peaceful, like medicine for the soul.

Grace looked over at Lily and said, "I love the beach. It is so calming. Since I have been working at the hobby store, I have always been drawn to the paint section. I have never tried to draw or paint, but I think I would like to try. I would love to capture this view on canvas so as to keep it with me wherever I go."

Lily said, "That it is a very good idea! Everyone needs a hobby, something they can escape to, to have a good time and think about something other than work or other troubles going on in their life. You never know you just might be very good at it."

They sat there for a little while longer before going up to bed.

The next morning, the sun was out but a little cool, and even then, you could tell that it was going to be a beautiful day. Grace was the first one up and started the coffee and went out to sit on the balcony and enjoy the morning view. There were only a couple of people out on the beach, and the waters were fairly still. As she sat there, her mind drifted back to a happier time when they used to live on the beach in Charleston. Tears started rolling down her face, as she remembered the loving family she used to have—when she truly felt loved and wanted. That was the last time she ever felt that way.

Lily stood in the doorway and, seeing her emotion, did not want to intrude. She silently prayed as she went back in to get a cup of coffee. *Lord, only you know all the pain that is buried deep within her heart. Heal her, and when necessary, give me the words to say in order to comfort her and lead her to you. In Jesus's name, amen.* With that, she made her way back to the balcony and this time announced herself, "Good morning! Isn't this view breathtaking?"

Grace, wiping the tears from her eyes, replied, "Oh yes, and very calming. Thank you, Lily, I needed this. It feels good and odd at the same time. I don't think I have ever done anything on the spur of the moment like this. Since being with Bobby at such a young age, I have not been able to make even one decision on my own. He had to approve and be in control of everything. It is sort of like stepping out onto new ground, and I am totally unaware of what lies beneath and wondering if I am going to sink or not."

Lily looked over at her and, with a gentle smile, said, "Grace, don't worry. You are going to be all right. You will find this new life you are stepping into will be quite liberating and invigorating at the same time. You are about to learn the joy that comes from being free and independent and making your own choices. If you succeed in those choices, good. If not, it is okay. Use the failures as lessons learned, and try again. It is not bad to make a wrong choice. Just learn and move on and rejoice in the good ones."

"Thank you, Lily. You are a good friend, and I really cherish your friendship. I don't know what I would do without you. It is as if you were brought into my life just at the right time," Grace said with a grateful look on her face.

Lily, looking out over the waves rolling in, said, "Grace, that is exactly it, and you will learn more and more about that as your heart is healed. For now, just enjoy yourself and think of me as an adopted sister!"

"Sounds good to me," Grace replied.

Lily finished her coffee, then said, "Come on, let's get dressed and get some breakfast! My stomach is beginning to growl angrily at me. It thinks I'm starving it!" They both laughed and agreed and were dressed and out the door.

After breakfast, since it was still a little cool, they decided to walk the Grand Strand and visit all the shops. They were like little girls as they went from shop to shop. This was wonderful medicine for Grace's soul. Grace looked over at Lily with a look of pure joy. Lily had never seen this in her before and was sensing that maybe she was beginning to relax; and the idea of being on her own, being her own person, was starting to sink in a little.

Running into the next shop, Grace raised both hands in the air and shouted, "What more can a girl ask for? The sun, the beach, and shopping!" Then she darted into the next gift shop as if she was racing.

Lily laughed along with her and ran alongside her as if she was up for the challenge. They walked and shopped and visited the sites for hours. It was already lunchtime, so they decided to get some lunch before heading back to the hotel to change for the beach!

By the time they reached the beach, it was full of people. They found a good spot to lay out their towels and their cooler. They sat for a while and watched everyone walking to and fro down the beach and the children splashing. Grace bought a travel magazine in one of the stores they went to and pulled it out to look at the beautiful pictures of different places and landscapes.

Lily took out a book she was reading by Joyce Meyers, her favorite author. It was called Beauty for Ashes. Grace glanced over at her and asked about it. Lily knew it was not quite time yet and gave her as short an answer as she could without being too detailed. "Joyce is one of my favorite authors. You name it. She has been through it and has come through it swimmingly! She has wonderful and inspired advice. I love reading her books. They are written with the wisdom she learned through experience."

She could see that an interest had sparked inside of Grace, but as suspected, she was not ready to tackle the subject of her pain quite yet. It was as if she was just home from the hospital and still recuperating from broken legs. She was not ready to try walking just yet.

The beach was full of life. Kids were playing in the water, splashing all around, others were playing volleyball, and still others were enjoying the sun as they were lying on their towels. Grace was captivated by the pictures in the travel magazine and looked over at Lily and said, "You know this magazine has inspired me to take a photography class. I think that I am going to look into it when we get back. I love the pictures of the different landscapes that are displayed in this magazine. I would love to be able to take pictures like this."

Lily replied, "That would be a great idea, and you might just be very good at it. It might even turn into a career for you one day."

A look of wonder and hope-filled Grace's eyes, and she pondered that and continued to look at the magazine. The girls continued to lay out in the sun and enjoyed being able to do whatever they wanted and not have to be anywhere at any specific time. Lily could see that this was indeed just what Grace needed to transition her into a new beginning.

After staying a bit more in the sun and enjoying the water along with everyone else out on the beach, the girls decided to come in and get dressed for dinner.

Afterward, they sat out on their balcony and watched the sun go down beyond the water. It was a beautiful sight as they looked upon the glimmer of the dimming sun fade away.

Grace sat there and thought, *I am going to paint this one day and capture the peace that these waters display—the peace that I finally feel inside. I would love to share that with the world, and one day, I am going to move here. I would love to wake up to the peace that this view gives me every day.*

5

∽

Starting Over and Memories Surface

Grace took some beautiful pictures. She drove through all the sights and back roads of Cherokee and even stopped to get some apples for her and Mr. Henry. She thought the pictures I took of the Blue Ridge Parkway turned out especially good. It was a successful venture and a nice little mini-vacation. I think my editor will be well pleased. Then she looked up, closed her eyes and prayed, "Lord, thank you so much. You have brought me so far and healed all that was broken inside—broken in areas I wasn't even aware of. Thank you for loving me and delivering me, even when I didn't know you existed. Thank you, Father, for loving me and inspiring me to seek out a career in photography. Capturing natural beauty through pictures is as if I am sharing a little bit of heaven's Grace in each picture I take. Thank you, Lord. In Jesus's name, amen."

At that, Grace packed up her things and started back home. It would be a long and tiring drive, but the pictures were worth the trip. As she drove back, her mind drifted back in time again to her first trip to Myrtle Beach, and she remembered how much she loved it there, and it was there that she had decided to look into photography. It was during her trip to Myrtle Beach with Lily right after what would be her last fight with

Bobby that she discovered what it felt like to be carefree. She discovered what it was like to not have to walk around on eggshells or to be afraid of everything she did or said that he might take it wrong and beat her again. It was the first time she had felt peace, and she decided right then that one day she would move to Myrtle Beach. She would look over the ocean and watch the waves roll in, and their beauty and wonder filled her with awe, and peace overwhelmed her heart. She never wanted to forget that feeling.

******

Driving back home, Lily and Grace talked and talked. They talked about their fun on the beach, their walks on the Grand Strand, and even some of the beachwear. They could not believe what some girls wear! They were having a wonderful time and grew even closer that weekend. The drive was long, and since Lily was driving, Grace fell asleep.

Lily looked over at Grace as she slept and thought, *I know that she will have many issues to overcome in healing her heart from all the abuse, but seeing her this weekend full of so much peace was nice. The old Grace screamed someone full of fear as much as she tried to hide it. Even though she is just starting her new life of freedom, seeing her this weekend having fun and the peace she had sure is heartwarming.*

They only had thirty minutes left in their drive home when Grace finally woke up. Lily looked over at her and said, "Well, nice to have you up, sleepyhead!"

"Where are we?" Grace asked.

"We are only thirty minutes away. You planned this, didn't you? So I would have to do all the driving!" Lily replied, laughing and giving Grace a sarcastic look.

"Oh, you caught me." Grace laughed back.

They talked about their weekend the rest of the way home. As they drove up into Lily's driveway, Grace looked over at her and said, "Well, we are home, and I guess life begins."

With a gentle look, Lily replied, "Don't worry. It will be okay. You will see that sifting through the emotions and figuring out your next moves will not be so bad, because you have someone who cares for support, me. Just take one step at a time. Don't feel as if you have to rush things. You can stay here as long as you need."

"Thank you, Lily," Grace continued. "I sure appreciate that, because right now, I don't know where to begin, but the beach really helped. The rest, the fun, and not thinking about anything helped to calm my mind a lot."

The next day was Monday, and they both had to work. Grace decided to take Lily's advice and take things one at a time. Grace filed for divorce, and given Bobby's attitude and the fact that he was in jail, she did not expect him to respond. She was sure that in his mind, if there is no response, there is no divorce. However in South Carolina, if after thirty days he does not respond, then it is considered a Default, and proceedings can begin to set a court date and finalize. That would be one step completed in starting over.

She filed for divorce on the grounds of physical cruelty, and in South Carolina, a year's separation is not required when filing under these circumstances. The date was set to finalize the divorce a year and one month from the filing date.

******

During her lunch break one day, Grace decided to open a savings account to save for a place of her own and to buy a camera and photography equipment. Grace was starting to feel alive again and beginning to have desires within for something fun. This was new to her and it made her feel good. The deep-rooted pain was still in her heart, but she was moving forward.

The travel magazine had truly inspired her, and she was determined to take photography classes. She also wanted to take art classes. The thought of being able to capture a beautiful landscape setting on canvas with a twist of how she interprets it, had also captured her interest. These were only external steps; but the ones most important, tackling her inward emotions, were yet to be examined. She was quite aware that she had issues but did not know the depth of them. One that she was sure of was the deep-seated fear she had within, and she knew she needed to get rid of it but did not know how.

When Grace and Lily got home from work, Grace began looking for classes on photography and art. There was a school nearby that offered both, and the length of the classes varied, depending on what she wanted to learn and the degree offered. She wanted to learn all aspects of digital photography, and the class lasted eighteen months. She wanted to learn but did not want a degree just yet. She also found an art class. Tuition wasn't bad and she found out all she would need for both classes. So the process of saving for the tuition and equipment was the first step; then she would register for the classes. Lily was truly impressed at Grace's determination and quite proud of her.

It seemed as if Grace was doing okay, but actually, she was just going through the motions. Internally, she was still a mess. The one thing that did clear up a long time ago, was the drinking problem that began when she was a teenager. Bobby put a stop to that after they married. Believe it or not, he would not have his wife become an alcoholic, and that was the only good thing that did come out of their relationship. However, there were more issues—the depression, the eating disorder, the fear of everyone wanting to hurt her, the fear of not doing anything right. There was also the needing to make everyone happy and overall worthlessness and insecurity, and she was still a long way off from being healed. It would be a process of her recognizing and seeking counseling for some issues and believing the truth behind all the lies she has believed about herself all these years. All these issues had created a wall around her that Grace has shut everyone, besides Lily, out for fear of being hurt. Even though Bobby was in jail, Grace walked around harboring the emotions she displayed while still with him. Myrtle

The beach was wonderful medicine for Grace, but when she returned to day-to-day life, the old Grace came back rather quickly. As Lily prayed, the Lord spoke to her, saying, "Just love her and be patient with her.

Listen to my voice directing you. You will know when to speak and when to offer a shoulder."

That night, Grace could not sleep. She had continual nightmares. It seemed that now that she did not have to be afraid of Bobby, it allowed freedom in her mind for memories to start slipping through, and she woke up screaming!

Lily came running into her room. "Grace, Grace, are you okay?"

Grace sat up on the bed crying and crying and spoke up. "It was so awful. I can't believe it! No! No! Not my dad! No!"

Lily asked, "What is it?"

"I can't talk. I just don't know. I can't remember," Grace replied.

Lily sat there and told her not to worry and that she would stay there with her until she fell back to sleep. She told her that it would be all right and that, whatever was trying to work its way through, she was okay now. It was a memory of what was in the past and could not hurt her anymore. She told her that when she was ready, she would be there to listen. Grace sat there with Lily for a while and cried herself back to sleep.

As Lily left the room, she silently prayed, "Oh Lord, I know Grace has been through something horrible. Please give me the wisdom to know how to lead her to you, to your healing love. In Jesus's name, amen."

As the weeks went by, the nightmares continued; and Grace's mood, which Lily had thought should have been better since becoming free of Bobby, had actually become worse. Anger was exploding from her and was starting to affect her demeanor. Unbeknownst to Lily, the memory of her dad's actions was so painful for her to accept as a child, so she buried them deep within her mind, and now they were surfacing. She was also having nightmares about her mom—nightmares of her mom yelling at her and slapping her.

She would cry out, "Mommy, Mommy, why are you mad at me?" In the dream, her mom would yell back, "It is all your fault, your fault," and keep hitting her. It was too much to bear, and she continued to cry every night. She could not talk about it, because she did not believe it herself. Why were these memories coming back now?

Grace mentioned to Lily that she was having nightmares about her mom and dad, but could not talk about them because she did not understand them. She did not know what to do.

Lily said, "I know that you have been estranged from your mom, but have you thought about asking her? She might be the only one who can give you some answers."

She had not seen her mother for a long time, but she knew she had to talk to her.

Grace reluctantly shook her head and said, "I guess that is the only answer."

She could not take any more of these dreams. She needed to get some sleep. She was feeling tired all the time lately. The memories of her past—the past forcing its way into the forefront of her mind and trying to deal with the emotional scars Bobby had left on her heart—were just too much.

She mentioned this to Lily, saying, "Lily, it is just too much for me. I don't know how to handle it, and I feel as if I am losing control."

Lily spoke up, knowing it was time. "Grace, it seems as if you had been through something very traumatic as a child, and with all the abuse of the present, it is just too much. I think you need to see a counselor who is experienced in this and knows how to walk you through your memories to help you face them and then let them go."

Reluctantly, Grace agreed, and she decided to set up an appointment on her next day off. She thought she would see the counselor first, before going to talk to her mother. Lily gave her the number of a Christian counselor who went to the same church. She had told her everything she knew about Grace, even the fact that she was not saved so Marion, her friend, would know how to approach things.

Grace went to see Marion and really liked her. She thought that she was very nice and seemed very understanding of her needs. Marion told her that she wanted to see her a couple of times alone. This was to get a clear picture of her emotional state now, the dreams she was having, and the physical issues as well before she talked to her mother.

Marion usually prays at the beginning and end of each session with her clients if they are willing. Since Grace was not saved, she decided to work that part in slowly, so she would not frighten Grace away.

Marion explained to Grace that everyone is different and how she works through things with her may not be the same for someone else. She wanted her and Grace to get to know each other first and become comfortable with each other, before they brought anyone new into the counseling sessions. She advised her not to talk to her mom just yet, but to wait to do it with her present. Marion also suggested to Grace to get a journal and whenever she felt depressed, angry, scared, etc., to journal it. She told her to write it down, along with what she was doing and what she was thinking about at the time and the emotion she was feeling. She also asked her to write down her first painful memory in life and the emotions she was feeling at the time, and they would discuss it on her next visit afterward.

Grace agreed, and it had been a few weeks so far, and Marion was dealing with the anger and discovered her anorexia problem. The journaling helped a lot. Marion would use the journals and what she felt would help her to go back to any other time when she had felt that same way. They would discuss it, and Marion would lead her to the truth regarding the feelings.

She explained that the anger was a normal emotion of her inner self, being mad at the things she had suffered. She explained to her that she needed to let it out, but in a healthy way and gave her some ideas; one idea being to get an oversized stuffed animal and to take out her anger on it, rather than letting it surface at others who are not the real cause of the anger.

It helped, Grace had said, and she also helped Grace to see that the eating disorder, was her way of controlling something about herself when she had been controlled by others for so long. She hadn't been in control of her own life since she was a child and then into her marriage. She helped her see through an exercise that whatever had happened, she had not asked for it to happen to her, so it was not her fault.

Grace was beginning to face that whatever happened in her childhood was not her fault and was even beginning to eat normally.

Lily was noticing the change and the well-needed weight gain, but she knew as well, that it was still going to be a long road ahead before the true healing took effect. She knew that it would not come without knowing Jesus. Lily knew that time as well would come. Jesus came to save and to heal and restore, and she needed to be patient and wait for the Lord's leading.

"But I will restore you to health and heal your wounds," declares the Lord, "because you are called an outcast, Zion for whom no one cares."
—Jeremiah 30:17

6

∽

Memories Examined One-by-One

Back home again! Grace had enjoyed her trip to the mountains and took some beautiful pictures, but it was nice to be home. Mr. Henry loved the apples and said he did not mind a bit taking care of her house; he was glad to do it.

Grace unpacked, and the sun was going down, just beyond the ocean waters. It left a dramatic glow across the water. Grace loved her little part of the beach, and the calmness and serenity that she drew from it always invited the presence of the Lord. It was her favorite place to sit and talk to Him.

She prayed again, "Lord, I sure do thank you for what you have brought me to and brought me through. I could not have done it without you. I know now, looking back, that it was you all along who directed my steps with the people you brought into my life, especially Lily, who were your instruments of love. Thank you so much."

"A man's steps are directed by the Lord. How then can anyone understand their own way" Proverbs 20:24"

As she sat there taking in the beauty of the still waters, her mind once again drifted back in time.

******

It had been almost two months now that Grace was seeing Marion. They discussed the dreams and her journals and what they meant. Although she knew something very bad had happened to her as a little girl, she still was not ready to face it. Grace was feeling better. She was no longer as depressed, and although she still did not understand why it started, she had conquered her anorexia. Although the anger would not totally go away until the painful memories of the past were addressed, she had found an outlet so as not to take it out on innocent people.

Marion said that it was time to start addressing the past and had set up a time for her to talk to her with her mother. It was a phone call she was not looking forward to, but knew if she wanted to get well, it needed to be done.

"Mom, it's Grace. I know it has been a very long time since I have talked to you, but so much has happened, and I am not well, emotionally. I married Bobby, and he was abusing me. He is in jail now, but I have a lot to work through."

Jennifer, with tears rolling down her face at the joy of hearing Grace's voice once again, spoke up. "Grace, I don't care how long it has been. I am truly sorry for the pain I have caused you. I had let the anger out at the wrong person. I was so angry I could not control it. I have sought help, and now I understand and wish I could take back all those years of pain I caused you, either directly or indirectly. I am so sorry, and if you give me half the chance, I would love to make it up to you."

"Mom," Grace started in, "that is just it. Bobby is in jail, and I am seeing a counselor. I do not remember what happened to me as a child. I guess the pain was just too much, and I blocked it out. The memories are starting to surface. I have been having nightmares, and the counselor wants me to hear the truth with you present at one of our sessions, so she can help me to process it and walk me through it. Will you come?" Sobbing now, she could not hold it back anymore.

Jennifer replied, "Of course, honey, anytime. I will do anything to get you back into my life."

With that and the time agreed upon, they hung up. Grace did not have all the facts, and although her mom seemed sincere, she still had anger and was not ready to forgive her mom, but she knew she needed her back in her life.

******

The day was finally here, and Grace was nervous about seeing her mom. It had been a very long time, but Grace was determined to get past the pain, at the thought of being normal and happy. Grace hesitated as she entered Marion's office, and the fear of facing the pain of her past had her almost frozen in her shoes.

Marion looked over at her and said, "Relax, Grace. It will be all right. Remember, the past is gone, and so are those that hurt you, and whatever memories surface are only memories."

Loosening up a bit, Grace sat down and replied, "Thank you. I needed that little reminder. I guess I am scared of what I will have to face and accept. It was evidently so bad that I blocked it out, and I am a little apprehensive about coming face-to-face with it."

"Just remember," Marion began, "I am here to walk you through, and I will not let it go too far beyond what you can bear right now."

"Thank you. That makes me feel a lot better," Grace said, a little more relaxed.

Marion began again, "Grace if you don't mind, I would like to pray before I begin. Is that okay with you?"

Grace replied, "I never have, but I guess that would be okay."

Marion was relieved, because she knew inviting the Lord into the pain was the only way of deliverance from it. The moment was here, and even though Grace was a little bit more relaxed, she still looked quite frozen, as her mother entered the room. They exchanged hellos and sat down across from each other.

Marion began, and looking at Jennifer, she said, "I don't want to rush into anything, and if Grace becomes too agitated, I am going to have to ask you to stop. Is that okay?"

Jennifer shook her head in agreement.

Marion continued, "Jennifer, this session, and more if needed, is to not only help Grace remember her past but to hear your side and bring healing and forgiveness to both of you, as well. Grace, please allow your mother to speak through without interrupting. Everyone is different and has different emotions and views of events. People react according to how 'they' perceive things to be. You may have seen things one way and your mom a different way. I am here to get to the truth and to help you to process it. Wrong or right, your mother has feelings too, and it may help you to understand her. Is that okay?"

Grace nodded her head in agreement, and Marion continued, "Jennifer, I want you to go back in time to when Grace was a child and at your first memory of something happening to Grace. Be honest without any accusing. Just state facts, and Grace, whatever she says is in the past and it cannot hurt you anymore. Now I would like to pray before we start. Father, I thank you for bringing Grace into my life, that you may help her through me. Give me the wisdom and the words that Grace needs to hear and reveal, and open Grace's eyes to the truth while holding her heart in your hands and keeping her strong. In Jesus's name, amen. Now, Jennifer, you may begin."

Jennifer began to cry. It had been a long time, and she thought that, by being saved, she had worked through all the pain she felt. This clearly showed that she had not, but how could it, when her little girl had been hurt and out of her life since it all happened?

Wiping the tears from her eyes, Jennifer began, "Grace was only seven years old when her dad was arrested, and we got divorced. Everything happened so fast after I found out what was going on. Believe me, I loved my girls very much, and I was completely blind to what Mark had been doing, and as soon as I found out, I made him leave. According to the doctor's examination, after Mark's arrest, they said it must have been going on for at least two years. I could not believe it! I was stunned at what was happening under my roof to my little girl. As a mom, I am supposed to protect my little children, and I failed miserably! I could not handle it or process it at all. It was as if all of a sudden a tornado came through and swept my family away." Jennifer was sobbing and cried out, "I am so sorry. I am so sorry, Grace. I am so sorry!"

"What?" Grace yelled out. "What, what did he do?"

Jennifer wiped her eyes and began again, "Grace, your father had been molesting you. I did not know he was doing it."

Before she could finish, Grace cried out, "No, no! He couldn't have! No!" She sat there and cried and cried while Marion held her.

After about thirty minutes, she finally calmed down, and Marion asked her, "Grace, will you be okay? We can continue tomorrow if you like?"

"No, Marion, I want to finish. I'm okay now."

Marion went on to say, "Grace, it may be hard for you to believe right now, but if it indeed happened, your memories may begin to surface. Hearing this and seeing the emotions that you exhibit and the other troubles you are having align with someone who had not only suffered from the present physical abuse but also the sexual abuse as a child. Jennifer, go on."

Jennifer, with heartfelt sorrow in her eyes, looked over at Grace and went on to say, "I had no idea it was happening. We had been having trouble since we moved from Charleston to Columbia. He had been going out a lot and coming home drunk. The smell of him made me sick, and I wanted nothing to do with him. He began sleeping on the sofa. I am usually a sound sleeper, so I never heard him when he came in until one night when I had a headache and could not sleep. I got up and went into Grace's room, and that is where I found him passed out on top of her! I could not believe it. I screamed at him to get out! He was too drunk to fight, and he sped out of the house and down the road.

I went to the police, and they had doctors examine Grace, and he was arrested. The emotions of it all came crashing down on me. I did not have a job or a husband anymore to provide for us. I had to find a job, find someone to help take care of the girls while I worked, and deal with the pain of what had happened to Grace. It happened all at once, and I did not deal with it very well and did not know how. This was a new subject to me. I did not have anything like this in my family, and I felt completely lost and alone. I felt guilty as well, that my little girl was being abused in that way and right under my nose. I handled it badly. I was angry, and the source of my anger was in jail, but for some reason, I blamed Grace and took it out on her. I know it was not her fault. She was a little girl, but I was so angry, ashamed, and full of guilt because of what had happened, and I was scared, all at the same time. I could not handle my emotions.

I got a hold of myself later and tried to apologize to Grace, and it stopped. I knew the damage was done. And she became distant, quiet, and subdued. I should have sent her to counseling, but I was trying to come to terms with all the emotions I was dealing with and could not see past them to see what she needed."

They were both sobbing now, and Jennifer could not help it any longer. She loved her daughter and missed her terribly and was different now that she had found Jesus. All she wanted to do now was to love her daughter's pain away. She ran over to her and held her and cried out,

"Grace, I am truly sorry, and I was so wrong. I didn't really blame you, but I could not handle everything that was happening and it was all at once. It exploded within me and unfortunately onto you. I am so sorry for how I blamed you and beat you because of it. Please forgive me."

Grace was crying as much as Jennifer, and although she was angry and hurt, she really needed a mom again, and dealing with what she had just heard about her dad was just too much. She knew she would need someone more than Lily and Marion to help her deal with it. She needed her mom again.

With both of them crying and hugging, Grace replied, "I forgive you, Mom. I missed you and have so much to tell you."

Marion went over a few more details and talked a little more, telling Grace to remember to journal, especially now. It would be very important, and she asked her to call her if she needed her. She set their next appointment, which would be next week unless Grace needed it sooner.

Grace and Jennifer walked out of the office together arm and arm. Grace had her mom back in her life again.

Marion, although she was a counselor, was a Christian first; and she knew that Grace would need the Lord to help her grasp all of this and to receive healing from it.

After the session, Marion prayed, "Dear Lord, please help this child, draw her to you, and heal her heart. I know, Lord, in your Word, Psalm 34:18, you promise, 'The Lord is close to the brokenhearted and saves those who are crushed in spirit.'"

7

Introduced to Jesus

The editor of the travel magazine loved Grace's pictures, and in fact, they were going to devote six pages in their next issue, *Fall in the Blue Ridge Mountains*, and use all of her pictures! Grace was so excited! She could not wait to get home and tell Mr. Henry.

It was Saturday, and you could tell that winter was trying to force its way through. It was very cold out, but that would not stop Grace from having her morning coffee and devotion time out on her porch. The wind was blowing, and it was really causing a stir over the waters of the ocean. The waves were continually rolling in, and as she sat there, she prayed and talked to the Lord. The force of the waves caused her mind to drift back once again to the force of emotions that flooded her mind and heart that night after she talked to her mom after so many years apart. They seemed to come at her all at once.

******

Grace and her mom went to a nearby café and sat in the corner where it would be private. They talked and talked. It was easier than she thought it would be to let go of her anger at her mom. She thought about the flood of emotions that would come at her all at once and the anger she felt toward Bobby and the fear while still with him. She understood how sometimes you cannot control your actions when that happens. Grace hugged her and told her she forgave her and she understood. Grace told her about her life with Bobby and how she started seeing Marion to help her come to grips with everything because her emotions were overwhelming her.

"Mom," Grace continued their conversation, "I do forgive you, and I understand, and I guess I have missed you and needed you more than I would let myself accept. How is Jolisa?"

Jennifer replied, "Jolisa just started attending the University of South Carolina. She wants to be a nurse. I am so proud of her, and she is very worried about you. She has missed you. Being so much younger than you when everything happened and your leaving made her feel as if you and she never really got to know each other. Maybe now that will change."

Grace shook her head in agreement. "I would like that, and I want both of you to meet Lily. She has been a real blessing and is the main reason I was able to leave Bobby."

"She sounds like a jewel," Jennifer replied. "I would love to meet her, and I want you to meet Sam. You were dealing with too much to really get to know him when you left and too much that I am sorry for and I was not aware. He is the one who was instrumental in my healing from the issues with your dad and the anger I felt and led me to the one who could heal me completely, Jesus."

Grace looked at her and said, "Just who is Jesus? I know Marion prays, but what is praying? I agreed in the session, but did not really understand."

Jennifer looked gently into her daughter's eyes and said, "I am sorry that I never talked about Jesus to you as a child, but I never grew up believing or hearing about Him either.

Grace, the world did not just appear—just as the watch on your arm didn't. It has a watchmaker, and the world has a Creator, God, and Jesus is his Son. Jesus is the Son of God, who came into the world to save it from their sin. God is holy, and mankind is truly corrupt and sinful on their own, 'For all fall short of the glory of God.' God knew that man could not repent of the sin on his own, so he sent Jesus to do that.

John 3:16 says, 'For God so loved the world that he gave his one and only Son, that whoever believes in him shall not perish but have eternal life.' He died for our sins, and whoever believes and receives Him receives His Holy Spirit which we are able to receive due to his death on the cross and rising to His glory in heaven back with His Father. Jesus is love and perfection. And with His Spirit within you, he is able to reveal, heal, guide, and deliver, and with you reading the Bible. It is His story.

I learned about who he really is to the world and to me through reading the Bible. I have also learned more in attending church with Sam. We go to a wonderful church, and maybe you can go with us sometime, honey."

Jennifer pulled a Bible out of her purse, "Please take this. I have another one. Read it. You may not understand all of this, but I promise if you do read it, you will understand. God wants everyone saved and to know him. The Bible says in 1 Timothy 2:3–4, 'This is good, and pleases God our Savior, who wants all people to be saved and to come to a knowledge of the truth.' And prayer is our way of communicating, talking to God just like you and I are doing now. It is getting late, and I have to go, but please call me, and maybe this weekend, you can come over and bring Lily."

Grace looked up at her with a look that said she was completely over-whelmed and did not have a clue about all of this and said, "I do not understand any of this, but I have wondered what church was. Lily goes every Sunday. I asked her one day, but I had been extremely depressed, and I guess she knew I needed more time to process what I had been dealing with and did not want to bombard me. She told me she would take me one day if I wanted to come and could find out then. I did not understand, but I agreed. I would like to come over, and, yes, Jolisa and I do need to get to know each other. I would like that. I will call you."

They hugged each other and went on their way.

******

That night, as Grace lay in bed, the memories of what her mom had said and the nightmares she was having bombarded her mind. Grace was in a state of shock, and so much so that the conversation she had with her mother about Jesus had gotten lost in the devastating news she just found out about her father. She was trying to process it all in her mind and started crying uncontrollably. She fell asleep holding onto her pillow as if for dear life. She knew it was all true.

The next day at work, Grace was even more subdued than usual, and Lily knew something had surfaced at her counseling session the night before and asked her on their break, "Grace, are you okay? You seem even quieter than usual."

Grace looked back at her and said, "Well, no, not really. I found out the reason for the nightmares I have been having. They are memories of something that really happened to me as a child. My mom was at the session, and believe it or not, I understood her actions, and I forgave her. We talked afterward, and she wants you and me to come for dinner this weekend. I would like that. I need to get to know my sister. I bet you didn't know I had one. She is a few years younger than me, and I was dealing with a lot of emotions in high school. At that time, they were overwhelming, and I did not understand why because I had blocked out my childhood and the things that happened. So in all of that, I really did not associate with my sister very much.

Her name is Jolisa, and I just found out that she just started attending the University of South Carolina. She is going to be a nurse. I am happy for her and even more that all the pain of our family did not seem to affect her. Nevertheless, I am fighting all the emotions bubbling up inside me, having to accept and believe what happened, the anger of it, the extreme pain in my heart of not having a dad and not having one that loved me as a dad should, the life that was stolen from me, and the need to be free of all the anger, pain, depression, and even the emotions I have had to just want to end it all. I have felt like everyone's punching bag. I seemed to attract the ones who wanted someone to be mean to and control me in ugly ways. It's not fair! Why me? Why me? Did I deserve this? What did I do as a child to deserve all of this?"

Grace was crying and crying now. Lily walked over to her and put her arm around her and said, "Honey, you did not ask for this, and you did not deserve this! Whatever happened as a child, you did not ask for any of this! Everyone is given free will, and what they choose to do or not do is their choice and no one's fault but their own! You were a child who was supposed to be loved and protected by your parents, and though you were not, it was not your fault! What the ones who hurt you chose to do is their fault, and what you choose to do now with the knowledge of what they did and how wrong it was, is your responsibility. You can work through your healing and let go, or you can choose to react in a bad way due to the pain you are feeling. If you do, then the responsibility for your actions is your fault. You can also allow them to continue to control you by holding onto the pain and anger and not forgiving. Don't let them destroy your life by holding onto the pain from it. Do not let what they put you through control the rest of your life through your emotions. Forgiving does not let the one who hurt you off the hook; it lets you off the hook from carrying around all that anger, pain, and sadness. As long as you carry that around with you, what they did is still controlling you. It was not your fault, so let yourself off the hook. Do not carry around guilt and shame for something you did not cause. Work with your counselor as she helps you to get rid of those bad emotions once and for all, and finally experience true happiness."

She paused and then continued.

"Everyone eventually reaps what they sow. You said your dad is in jail and did not know why. Well, I guess now you do, and he is paying the price for what he did. You suffered as a child and as an adult, and now the ones who hurt you are out of your life, and now it is your time to heal and to reap a blessing. It has already begun. You have your mom back in your life and are about to have your sister. You are going to counseling to be eventually healed and free emotionally and are even taking art and photography classes. It is your time, so keep going, and give it time. It will eventually be to your advantage."

Grace wiped her eyes. Their break was over. She looked at Lily and said, "Thank you, Lily. I am so grateful to have you in my life. You have been such a blessing."

They hugged and went back to work. Although it made Grace feel better at the moment, it did not change the Pandora's box of emotions she had within; she was either angry or depressed or just didn't care about life in general. The accomplishments she had made so far since being on her own have been merely going through the motions.

Grace couldn't sleep at all that night; the nightmares were even worse and even more graphic. Grace was beginning to remember more than just "a monster" trying to get her. That is what she kept dreaming of before—a big dark figure that kept trying to get her—and he would not stop, and he did not smell good either. Now she was getting more details in the dream. She wasn't sure if her mom had triggered memories, or if they were dreams based on what her mom had said. In any case, she still felt disconnected as if it had all happened to someone else. She hurt and was angry and didn't know why. Now she finds out from her mom the reason, but she still feels as if it was someone else's story.

Grace couldn't take it any longer and called Marion the next day to make an appointment to see her. Grace wrote nonstop in her journal just as Marion had asked, and it helped to get all her feelings down on paper.

An appointment was made and Grace went to see Marion. They prayed again at the beginning of their session, and they discussed her emotions and the things she remembered and had written in her journal. Marion also discussed her fears and told her that it was her fears that were keeping her from moving forward and the reason the monster in the dream did not have a face.

Marion did not want to go too fast with her. So for now they focused on her journal. They discussed the things she was feeling and what she was doing at the time to see if any particular actions were the trigger point to the emotions she was feeling. They discussed any memories she had of the first time she began feeling that particular way. Marion helped her to learn how to deal with her feelings and ask herself why she was feeling that way. The dreams still visited her every night. She needed a break from it and did not know how to get it.

When Grace got home that night, she plopped down on the sofa and looked as tired as she felt. She felt as if she had not slept in a week, and it was almost true.

Lily came over and sat down beside her and asked, "Grace, are you okay? I know you have been dealing with a lot lately, and it must be terribly hard to process it all. I'm here if you need me. You know that, don't you?"

Grace, was trying to look as if she was okay and said, "I know, and I do need you. My mom unloaded a lot on me, and it made sense with the dreams I had been having. It all seems true, but I still feel disconnected from it all. And I am angry, and it is more than what Bobby put me through. It seems as if the anger goes a lot deeper. I feel as if I am trying to walk through a maze blindfolded. I need a break from all these emotions. I have been going through the motions of life and trying not to fall apart, but I can't deal with it anymore."

Lily, trying to comfort Grace as she sobbed in her arms, knew she needed to do something to take her mind off it and reminded her of dinner with her mom.

Grace said, "Yeah that is a good idea. I will call her tomorrow. Thanks, Lily. It will be nice seeing my sister, and I can't wait for you to meet them."

******

It was Friday. Grace called her mom from work, and everything was set. They were going over to her mom's on Saturday. Grace was a little nervous about seeing her sister. Jolisa was just a kid when she last saw her and remembered very little of Sam, her mom's new husband, since she had moved out and gotten married at such a young age.

Grace came home from work and told Lily it was all set and was excited and a little nervous at the same time. It had been a while since she had seen her sister and did not know what to expect. Grace retired to her room early that night. Her emotions still overwhelmed her and was looking forward to going to her mom's if only to escape her personal reality for a bit.

******

It was a beautiful morning! The sun was shining, and the birds were chirping in the trees in Lily's front yard. The two had decided to do some yard work, and Grace was actually happy. Lily enjoyed seeing Grace smile and laugh. She had not done to much of that lately. They worked in the yard most of the day. The butterflies in Grace's stomach reappeared as she drove up to her mom's house.

"Lily, it has been so long, and even in making amends with my mom, I am still nervous."

Lily looked over at Grace and replied, "Grace, you were a child when all the bad took place with your mom. You said everything happened all at once and, like a bomb, she exploded, unable to handle it. You understood that, and having your dad arrested was proof of her love for you. It has been years, and you know she has changed. Your sister is grown and has probably missed you a great deal. I am sure she is looking forward to having her sister back in her life again. They are your family, and they love you, or your mom would not have wanted you to come. Family, when they truly love you, will love you for who you are, your faults as well as your accomplishments. You have nothing to be nervous about. Smile and be happy and enjoy not having to work today!"

They both laughed as they got out of the car and approached the front door.

Jolisa answered the front door, and Grace was amazed at how beautiful her sister had turned out. She had brunette hair, which was long and straight.

Jolisa smiled and threw her arms around Grace and said, "Welcome home, big sis! I have missed you so much!"

They stood there in the door and hugged for a while, and then Lily spoke up. "Are you forgetting someone?"

They all laughed as Grace introduced Lily, and they hugged some more and then walked into the living room to meet Sam.

Sam got up off the sofa and walked over to Grace. "Grace," he said as he hugged her gently, "I know you probably do not remember me, but I have always thought of you as my daughter and have prayed for you every day with your mom, and by the way, she just went upstairs. She will be down in a minute."

Grace pulled away, not realizing just how much she did not trust men, and said timidly, "Thank you, and you are correct. I do not remember much about you. My mind was in a fog back then. I think I walked around more like a zombie than someone truly alive. I hope to get to know you now."

They all sat down on the sofa and talked a bit more. Grace was a little anxious to find out just how much her sister knew about everything that was going on but did not want to rush into that conversation. She was still trying to process it herself.

Just then Jennifer came down, and grinning from ear to ear at the sight of Grace being in her home again, she ran up to Grace and threw her arms around her. Joyful tears began flowing from her eyes.

"Grace, I am so glad you are here. I have never stopped missing you or praying for you. I am so glad to have you back!"

"Mom," Grace began to say, "I am glad to be back, and thank you for having us, and by the way, this is Lily, and she is like a sister to me. She is the reason I am free from Bobby. Since I have met her, things just seemed to happen so fast it was as if she were an angel sent from heaven."

Tears welled up in both of their eyes as Grace looked at Lily affectionately.

"Thank you, Grace, I am so glad that I could help you. No one deserves to be treated the way Bobby was treating you."

Jennifer and Sam both thanked Lily, and Jennifer said,

"Lily, please think of yourself as part of the family."

They all sat for a few moments and talked and got caught up in what everyone was doing, and Jennifer was happy to know that Grace was taking classes.

Jennifer got up and excused herself, saying, "You all continue. I have to finish dinner."

Lily and Grace got up and in unison said, "Let us help."

"No, no, it is quite all right. You just make yourself at home. I can manage."

Lily continued, "Mrs. Morris, I would love to help if you don't mind."

"Well," Jennifer replied, "All right if you really want to. But, Grace, you stay and catch up with your sister."

They left the room, and Jolisa came to sit by Grace. "Sis, would you like to see the house? I know it has been a long time."

"Sure," Grace answered. They both walked to the house and ended up outside. They talked about Jolisa's school years, what she did, and that she graduated with honors. Grace was happy about that and even more excited about her going to the university.

"What made you go into nursing?" Grace asked.

"Well," Jolisa began, "Mom told me in my senior year what had happened to you. As I got older, I suspected something bad happened. I just put the pieces together, remembering Dad in prison and the day I caught you in the bathroom when you took those sleeping pills. I knew something had happened to you to make you do that. I just did not know what, and I thought it strange that I didn't hear anything about you after all these years. I kept questioning Mom, and she would dance around the subject and give me only enough to realize you have been hurt badly and were having trouble coming to grips with it. One day, I needed to know, angry that my sister was not in my life. I missed you and was angry! I know you are much older than me, but as I became a teenager, I felt that we could have finally become friends as well. I made Mom tell me. I was shocked and overwhelmed. I could not believe it. Since Sam has been in our life—he really is a good man—we have been going to church, and the pastor helped me a lot. I was able to let the anger go and forgive Mom, and even Dad. She even told me how she took the whole thing out on you. I know you were the one who was abused, but you are my sister, and although the things that happened to you stole our life together and being able to really get to know each other, I still loved you. I was angry and felt it happened to me as well. After that, I filled out the application to the University of South Carolina. I did not want to go into psychology but wanted something more hands-on to help people. So that is when I decided to go into nursing."

"Jolisa, I am so proud of you," Grace replied.

They hugged each other and talked some more about their likes and dislikes, and Grace even told her about her classes and how she wanted to paint. They all had a lot of fun, and Grace remembered something Jolisa said earlier about how the pastor had helped her to forgive. She wondered how. They had never been to church growing up and felt a little ignorant in not knowing what it was about. She knew Lily went and had seen churches, but that was all she knew about them. Lily spoke of it now and then, but her mind was too full of baggage to comprehend. Now she was beginning to get hungry for the knowledge of what it was all about. The thought of being able to let the pain within go and all the anger too was something she hoped for, but something she did not believe could happen. It had lived with her for far too long. Later that night, when Jolisa invited Grace and Lily to go out to the patio to talk, the thought still lingered in her mind.

She had to ask, "Jolisa, what did you mean by the pastor helping you to forgive, and I hate to ask, but what is a pastor exactly?"

Lily could not believe her ears! In her heart, she was shouting for joy, *Thank you, Father!*

Jolisa was astonished and gently began, "A pastor is someone who teaches and preaches about Jesus Christ, and a church is where he preaches from. It is the Temple of God in which we come together to praise and worship God, study the Bible, and learn about and draw people to Jesus. We the people within are the church, and the church building is where we meet. God is the Creator of the world and us. The watch you are wearing just did not appear in the store. There had to be a creator. God is spirit, and we are flesh. He created us to be His children. In our natural selves, we are weak, and just like any child, they do not always obey their parents. We do not always obey God or listen to His

Spirit's directions, and people get hurt like you did. The fault always remains with the one who disobeyed and not the parent and not God."

She pointed to a potted plant that had one stem of flowers growing out of it but three separate flowers.

She said, "There is one stem, one God. One stem but three flowers and one God but three separate just like the flower. Two other flowers are branched off from the one. This is the meaning of the Trinity, three in one: God the Father, God the Son, and God the Holy Spirit. Through God came Jesus Christ, and through Him, we have the Holy Spirit. With a Father and children, there always has to be discipline, and man's sins were just too great. There is a great price to pay for unrepeated sin, and that is eternal separation from God. Satan was an angel once and rebelled against God, and God cast him out. He is the one who makes trouble and leads people to sin against God and hurt others. Grace, you know that people die. Well, where do you think they go? There is heaven, which will be eternity with God, or hell, eternity with evil—the choice is ours. When the punishment for the gravity of the sin was too great, God knew he had to do something or all of his creation, us, would wind up in hell.

"He loved us too much for that. 'See what great love the Father has lavished on us, that we should be called children

Of God! And that is what we are.'" 1 John 3:1

So He sent Jesus, His one and only Son, to be the punishment for our sins.

'For God so loved the world that he gave his one and only Son, that whoever believes in him shall not perish but have eternal life' John 3:16.

Jesus came in the form of a man because it is man who sins, so it is a man who needs to be punished and needs to be one who is without sin. Jesus, the Son of God, had to be that punishment—that atonement.

'For we do not have a high priest who is unable to empathize with our weaknesses, but we have One who has been tempted in every way, just as we are—yet he did not sin' Hebrews 4:15.

They hung Him on the cross by God's will to be sacrificed for our sins.

'So Christ was sacrificed once to take away the sins of many' Hebrews 9:28.

The only way to receive the atonement that Jesus paid for by his death on the cross is to believe who he says he is and receive him. Ask him into your heart. Then you are saved and promised a home in heaven for eternity with God.

'If you declare with your mouth, "Jesus is Lord," and believe in your heart that God raised him from the dead, you will be saved. For it is with your heart that you believe and are justified, and it is with your mouth that you profess your faith and are saved.' Romans 10:9–10.

Grace, I know I gave you a lot more than you bargained for, but I could not tell you what a pastor is without telling you about the One for whom he is preaching about and why. 'The fear of the Lord is the beginning of knowledge.'

As you begin to read the Bible and pray, God will make it clear to you. The Bible is God's Word, and it contains his story of love and instructions for us. It is the story of Jesus, and to truly learn about who Jesus is, you need to read the Bible. Do you have one?"

"Yes, I do! I do!" Grace answered. "I was not sure what it was at the time, but Mom did give me one. How did that help you to forgive?"

Jolisa continued, "It helped me by the love of God in my heart. That same love that forgave me of my sins lives in my heart and is now able to help me to forgive those who wrong me. I just needed to ask God to help me, and he did. He gave me peace, an eternal peace that no natural thing can ever give or even compare. His love rose up from within my heart and gave me the strength to forgive and to let go. He will do that for you, and I know that by even the meaning of your name. Do you even know what your name means? The Greek word for Grace is Charis, meaning Grace, as a gift or blessing brought to man by Jesus Christ, favor, gratitude, thanks, kindness. Your name means 'Grace, favor, blessing, and kindness to men from God.' Grace, by the very meaning of your name, you are a blessing! God wants to heal you. Seek him out, and trust in his love to heal and lead you safely through to deliverance from all the anger and despair within."

By this time, it had been two hours, and all three of them were hugging and crying. This time, the tears that were rolling down Grace's face were tears that would lead to her healing. Both Sam and Jennifer were watching inconspicuously from right inside the patio door. Tears were rolling down their face as well. They looked at each other and said, "Praise God!"

Jennifer continued, "I did not know she listened in church that intently. I guess she did, and thank you, God, for using Jolisa to help lead her sister to you to make her whole and happy. Thank you so much, Father God!"

This is what the Lord, the God of your father David, says: I have heard your prayer and seen your tears; I will heal you. On the third day from now, you will go up to the temple of the Lord.
—2 Kings 20:5

8

∽

Learning to Forgive

November was blustering its way in. The winds had an icy feeling to it, and the waves rolling in from the ocean looked as if they were in an angry rush to roll into shore.

All this did not stop Grace from having her morning coffee and devotion time outside and watching the sunrise. This was her absolute favorite time of day. Grace was reading the Song of Solomon and was quite amazed at just how much she was beginning to love this particular book of the Bible. When she was initially saved, she could not read it. She still had issues within her heart and was having trouble believing just how much God loved her. She could not make herself read it and tried to once, but stopped and passed right over it. Now it was different.

God had healed her of so much, and she felt so content within that she wanted to read it. She had finally come to the realization of God's overwhelming love for her.

"I have loved you with an everlasting love. I have drawn you with loving-kindness."

Now she wondered, why did I ever want to pass this book by? It is such a beautiful love story—a love story between God and us, all who surrender to him. And every time Grace reads this book, the tears well up in her eyes with emotion at the gratefulness she feels and her overwhelming love for God. He has brought her through so much and was there all along even though she did not even know he existed.

Now she has a heart that has been made whole, and she has her family back in her life. Grace was even more excited because with Thanksgiving coming up she was going to host it at her house! Sam and her mom were coming, and Jolisa was spending the Thanksgiving holidays with her! Even Lily was coming! The whole family was going to be there! Lily, whose parents had died not long ago, had sort of been adopted by everyone. Jolisa called her, her other big sister. She never cared about the holidays before she was saved, but now she had so much to be thankful for; she cherished everyone who came around.

As she sat and read through her study, there was still a tugging at her heart that she could not get past. She knew the old memories were being dredged up for a reason and just did not know why yet. She remembered back when she first heard about Jesus. It was a little overwhelming.

******

With a rush of tears on the way home from her mom's house that first night back, she had voiced it to Lily. She felt a little stupid that her little sister seemed to "get it," and she just felt like crawling up in a corner. It sort of made sense, but at the same time, it was very confusing.

Lily and Grace said their goodbyes, and as Lily drove back home, Grace was thinking about the night and could not hold the tears back any longer. She began crying uncontrollably.

"What's wrong?" Lily asked.

"It's everything. It's just too much. It is the need to be whole and not in pain and the nightmares are gone and wanting to remember. At the same time, I am kind of scared to and desperately need peace in my heart—the kind of peace that Jolisa mentioned. My little sister seems to have more understanding than I do. I find it all so confusing, and at the same time, I want to know more. There is a glimmer of hope that if there is a God who loves so much and can heal my heart and take the pain away, I want to know him. At the same time, I am scared that maybe he does not exist, and the glimmer of hope is only futile. There is even more hope knowing that my name means a blessing to men by Jesus. Me, a blessing? How can that be? I have not felt like a blessing, but in learning what my name means, it gives me hope. I have hope that maybe if there is a God, just maybe he does want to heal me and give me joy in my heart. There is just too much going on in my mind and my heart, and I want it all to stop. I want to be loved, and I want to be happy, and I want so desperately to be able to trust people again and to believe that everyone is not out to hurt me."

Lily was quiet for a moment, overcome by everything that Grace had just poured out of her heart, and prayed silently, God, give me the words to console her without overwhelming her even more. Grace wiped the tears from her eyes as she began to settle down a little.

Lily spoke up, "Grace, you said a mouthful so to speak, and I am not putting that lightly. Grace, you are a joy, and it was people who hurt you and rejected God's command to not hurt his little girl, you. God put a light in you by the very meaning of your name, and those who hurt you tried to dim that light. Trust God to turn it back on and heal your heart and give you joy. They hurt you on their own, their fault, not yours. Don't try to rush in and 'get' everything all at once. Just take one thing at a time.

As Jolisa said, read the Bible your mom gave you, and God will show himself to you and open up your eyes to understand. In healing your heart, I think you said something back there without realizing that you did—something that will help you to remember. You said you were scared. Grace, you are scared to remember what happened. Your mom told you but only as a matter of fact, and that is why you do not remember, and you feel disconnected. You are scared to remember the details, the details that will make it real. Scared because it will hurt too much to know your dad did something so awful to you. The dad that was supposed to love and protect you hurt you and violated you instead. Remembering will open the door to revisit the situation and know what happened and, yes, the pain as well.

This time, it will be to accept that it happened, feel the pain, and then let it go. The only way to do that is like Jolisa said, to allow God into the situation to help you to forgive. Your therapist mentioned what the fears are doing, but she will help you to face what happened to you and deal with the pain and heartache caused by the abuse, but God will help you to forgive. Forgiving is not letting them off the hook. It is releasing the pain of what happened and the people who caused it into God's hands. I don't know about you, but I do believe God is much more powerful and can deal with them and make them see what they did to you in a much better way. God's love is unconditional, and only with his unconditional love can you in turn let go and forgive and in his strength, not yours."

Grace, much more calm now, looked over at Lily as they pulled into the driveway and said, "Lily, I know you are right. I have been scared, and that fear is so great within me that it has put up a wall inside me that has kept me from remembering. I am still too scared to face it. I want to, but I need help."

Lily asked her, "Would you be willing to allow Marion to try something new even though you are not sure right now about God? It is called prayer therapy, and she sits alone with you and calms your spirit first. This helps you to stop your mind so to speak and pray with you through your childhood memories until you get to the part with the bad memories in order to help you to remember. You take the memories one by one. I know it can help you, and it would be in a controlled environment with your therapist, and remember the memories are just that, memories.

Memories in themselves cannot hurt you, and facing them again can only help. You are facing them to let them go. Praying through with your therapist even though you are still unfamiliar with praying may even help you with that because, whether you understand that part or not, God is the Creator. He is also our heavenly Father, who loves you and is himself angry at the pain you suffered and wants to heal you. Marion, being a Christian counselor, can walk you through the pain and bad memories. This can be the breakthrough you have been waiting for. Please do not allow fear or lack of understanding to stop you now—not when you are so close and have come so far. You have overcome you're eating disorder, and you have made amends with your mom. Bobby is in jail, and the link to your breakthrough that will help with the depression and the anger and hopelessness is tied to facing the past."

Grace replied, as they went inside, "Thank you, Lily. You have helped to put things in the right perspective. I am scared, but I believe I am close to a breakthrough. So I am going to ask Marion next week about the prayer therapy, as you call it. I do not understand it, but I know I have walls around my heart—walls of fear—so I am just going to do it. I am going to do it afraid."

Lily smiled and said, "Grace, that is a huge step, and it is a step that takes great courage. You need to be proud of yourself. Courage is not the absence of fear or acting bravely without being afraid. It is taking action while being afraid."

Grace, needing to calm her mind a bit, prayed for the first time. As she sat there alone on her bed, she prayed,

"God, I know I have never prayed to you before, and I am not even sure you exist. This is all so new to me, but Jolisa said to ask, and, well, here I am asking. Please show yourself to me and help me to know that you do exist. I want you to because it will be nice to know there is a higher being out there more powerful than I am that will be on my side. It is also confusing. I don't know what to believe, but please help me. I am tired of all the heartache, and I don't want to be afraid anymore that everyone wants to hurt me. I want to believe in you and to trust you, so if you are listening, thank you."

She rolled over and felt a sense of peace and thought, Wow, me, a blessing? A gleam arose in her heart as she drifted off to sleep.

******

Grace woke up rested for a change and with no nightmares during the night! Monday, she decided she would call Marion about her next session so she could prepare for it. Marion was quite pleased that she even asked and was ready to remember. Grace also decided to take her camera with her to work. She wanted to go to the park and take some pictures. There was a park nearby, and Grace loved to go there and watch the birds in the trees and the kids playing. After work, she made sure she had all her camera equipment and got a few drinks and was off to the park. It was quiet today. There were not many people there. She found a nearby bench and set up her camera.

A bird caught her eye in a nearby tree, and the yellow in its wings was beautiful! She hurried to get the right shot before it flew away, and yes! Just in time! That would be a good one. Pleased with herself and thinking about the next shot she would take, Grace did not even realize the presence of an old woman who walked up beside her.

The old woman spoke up, "Excuse me, miss, can I bother you for one of those bottles of water? I have been here a while, and I did not think to bring one."

Grace was startled at first. She was lost in her thoughts about her pictures, and she whirled around to see this sweet- looking little old lady. She was short, between four and five feet tall, and had a kind, gentle look on her face.

"I'm sorry, ma'am. I was lost in my thoughts and did not realize you were there. Of course, you may." And Grace handed her one of the bottles. "My name is Grace. What is yours?"

The little old lady said as she sat down beside her, "My name is Christine."

"Oh, that is a beautiful name," Grace replied.

"How long have you been taking pictures?" the lady asked.

"Not long, I just started, and I have been taking classes too. I really enjoy it, and I think it is about capturing the beauty of the moment. That is what draws me to taking a certain picture."

"That is so wonderfully put. I have never heard it said like that."

Getting up to go on her way, she looked at Grace and said, "You are going to do that professionally one day. The art classes you are taking will entice your heart more than the photography classes. In fact, as you move to the beach, your first picture will be of the sun setting over the ocean. You will capture the peace and serenity, making the ones viewing it feel as if they are right there seeing it for themselves. Grace my dear, you are a blessing, and never let anyone tell you any different."

Overwhelmed about what Christine just said, Grace did not even notice her speed away. She tried to catch her breath and thank her, but she was gone. A joy seemed to fill Grace's heart as she looked up and prayed, "Thank you, God! You work fast! You do exist, and I know that now. I never mentioned painting to her, and she could only know that if you had told her. Thank you, and I believe in you now."

With tears of joy rolling down her face, she remembered the verse Jolisa had said about believing and confessing. So she sat there in the park and confessed her sins and that she believed in God and Jesus. She asked him to come into her heart, and she knew she was as Jolisa had said, saved. Before leaving, she asked God to help her understand the Bible and teach it to her, and help her with her upcoming session with Marion. She knew she still had some bridges to cross but now knew she had someone to help—Jesus. Grace could not wait to get home and tell Lily. She packed up her equipment and raced home.

Lily was sitting in the living room reading a book and looked up as Grace came in the door, shouting, "I did it. I did it!"

"What, what did you do?" Lily asked. Grace told her about the park and the little old lady and her prayer last night.

"Lily, she could not have known that. It was God answering my prayer and in a way special to me. He was letting me know he exists, and he heard my prayer. Not only that, I did it! I understand what saved means because I am saved! I did it! I confessed and asked Jesus into my heart and to help me with Marion next week. I did it, and I know his Spirit is in my heart. I feel him. I just know."

Lily was as excited for Grace as Grace was for herself! They both sat there and hugged and talked and then Lily spoke up, "Grace, you have to call your sister. Since she is the one who ignited the glimmer of hope in you and made you question, you have to tell her."

"You are right, and I'm going to do that right now!"

Grace replied.

Jolisa was ecstatic! They talked for a while on the phone, and she even told Jolisa about the prayer therapy session with Marion.

Jolisa comforted her, saying, "God has brought you this far. He will be with you in that as well and get you through it. He will never leave you nor forsake you."

They hung up, and Grace and Lily sat there and talked some more before eating dinner. That night, Grace pulled out the Bible that her mom had given her and began to read. Lily told her to start in the Book of John and read through the New Testament. She said that if she began there it would help her to understand the Old Testament because the Old Testament points to Jesus. There is so much symbolism of Jesus there. So you have to know him first to understand and to see the symbolism of him in the Old Testament. Grace could not get enough of it. If it were not for the weariness of her body, she would have read straight through the book of John, but as it was, she still read half. It was all making sense to her; she really believed, and peace filled her heart as she drifted off to sleep.

******

The day was here, and Grace had many mixed emotions about the session and what this "prayer therapy" was all about. She surprisingly enough asked her mother to join her at the approval of Marion. Grace was a ball of nerves; her fear was showing vividly. She was almost frozen as she met her mom at the door of the Marion's office.

"Grace, are you okay?" Jennifer asked. "You look like you are in a daze. Honey, it is going to be okay. Your dad is in prison, and he cannot hurt you anymore. The things that you will remember are only memories. It is going to be okay."

"I know, Mom," Grace replied. "I guess I don't want it to be real. I don't want the things I have imagined to be a reality. Now is the time that I have to face it, and I want to, but at the same time, I don't. Thinking my father could have done those things to me is a pain that I don't want to have to accept. Remembering them will make me have to, but I am ready. Let's go."

They walked in the door, and Marion greeted them and motioned Jennifer to sit on the other side of the room and to be extremely quiet during the session. She did not want any interruptions until they were through. She reminded Jennifer that she was only there for support if Grace became uncontrollable. Jennifer agreed, and Marion and Grace began their session by, first of all, praying and inviting the Holy Spirit into the session.

Marion put some soothing instrumental music on and asked Grace to sit and close her eyes and listen to the music. She then asked the Lord, "Please, dear Lord, take Grace back and help her to remember. Show her the truth step by step holding her, and keep her strong through it all, in Jesus's name, amen."

Marion started by talking about current events first and the past week —the things that happened and the realizations Grace had discovered. They talked about her fear, and most importantly, Grace told her about being saved and how that happened.

"I am so happy for you! My, but you truly have progressed! Grace, you don't know just how important that is, because the Lord can and will help you to face what you are about to face. Firefighters do not go into a burning building without the proper protection and gear. You now have the protection and strength within you to face your past. His strength within you will help you to face it. The Lord says in Philippians 4:13, 'I can do everything through him who gives me strength.' Now, are you ready to continue, and are you sure you want to go through with this? Are you ready to remember?"

"I guess as ready as I will ever be," Grace replied.

Marion prayed again with Grace and took her back to happier times, and by asking questions, she gradually moved her to the time right after they moved to West Columbia. She finally got to the time when the abuse began. Grace became very agitated, and Marion could tell she was very afraid. Grace, with eyes still closed as if she were there in that time period, started screaming so loudly Jennifer, as a reflex, started to run toward her.

Marion motioned to her to sit and whispered, "I have this. It is all right."

Continuing, Grace was screaming, "No, Daddy, no! I don't like this! No, Daddy!"

Marion began to speak to her, "Grace, you are remembering the past. It is a memory, and he is not here, and he cannot hurt you anymore. I am here and will keep you safe."

Grace started to calm down and said, "Okay, but I am afraid. Daddy is doing something to me he has never done before, and he smells funny. I don't like it, and the smell makes my stomach sick."

Marion continued to talk to her and prayed as Grace remembered more. "Lord, give Grace peace in her heart and let her know you are there with her. Show her the truth in order to overcome it."

"Grace, tell me, honey, what your daddy is doing."

Grace began again, and this time she was crying—tears flowing from her eyes. "Daddy, stop. I don't like this. Stop, Daddy."

Marion asked her again, "Grace, what is he doing?"

Grace replied as the tears rolled down her face, "Daddy is taking off my nightgown, and he is putting something in me, and I screamed, 'It hurts! It hurts! No, Daddy! No, stop!'"

Marion spoke up once again, "Grace, you are remembering the event that caused you so much pain and know now that it is only a memory. How old were you here?"

Grace replied, "I was five years old at that time."

Marion continued praying and talking to Grace, "Dear Lord, hold Grace tightly as she remembers the things her dad did, and help her to let it go. Grace, your dad is gone now. What are you feeling?"

Grace answered, "Scared and angry. Why did he do that? I felt dirty and ugly inside, not as good as other people."

Marion answered, "Grace, it is okay to feel angry about that. Dear child, you are not ugly, and we are going to ask the Lord to remove that pain and the feeling of being dirty and unclean. Dear Lord, we come to you now and ask you to help Grace and please heal her heart. Help her to release the pain to you so you can remove it, and let the cool rain of your love sweep through her heart and cleanse her. Help her to see herself as the beautiful princess and child of the King that she is, in Jesus's name, amen. Grace, did your dad ever hurt you like that again?"

Grace answered back, "Yes, and I tried to make him stop, but he wouldn't, and he even told me not to tell anyone, or they would be mad at me. He did this every week for a long time."

Marion asked again, "Grace, how old were you when he stopped coming in?"

Grace replied, "I had just turned seven years old. Why did he hurt me like that? Why? What did I do? Was I bad?"

Grace was sobbing profusely as Marion spoke up,

"Grace, the Lord directs all of us, and it is our fault and not God's and not the person being hurt if we do not listen. You did not ask for anything. You were a little girl.

Dear Lord, I pray that you continue to guard Grace's heart and bring healing from the pain, and remove it. Help her to give it all to you now that she knows it and fill her with your peace, in Jesus's name, amen."

Grace just sat there, and the tears flowed even heavier than before. Marion motioned for Jennifer, who at this time was crying along with Grace.

Jennifer came to sit beside Grace, and she just held her and told her, "Grace, I am so sorry. I truly had no idea he had been doing that to you for so long. I am so sorry, honey! Grace, just as Marion said, you were a little girl and your dad was bad. He was the one who was wrong. He chose to do that to you, and you did not make him."

She sat there and held her for a little while until Grace had calmed down.

After Grace had calmed down, Marion began to speak again, "Grace, do you remember everything now?"

"Yes, Marion. I remember it all. It hurts so much! He was my dad! Why did he do that?" Grace said, still crying.

Marion replied, "Grace, we may never know why he did what he did to you. He was messed up, and from what you and your mother had told me about him before you moved to Columbia, he was a good father. He just got messed up, and sick mentally. It does not compare, but you have been hurt. Because of that, you have had a lot of anger and depression, and other issues. Something like that happened to him, and because of that, he became sick and did what he did. He is in prison now, and he has to see a psychologist as part of his sentence. He will get the help he needs. Remember, Grace, he chose to do this to you. You were a little girl, and you did not ask for it, and you did nothing wrong to make him do it. This was his fault and his alone. You were a precious little girl. You have nothing to be ashamed of or fear anymore. It is over, and you are a beautiful young woman with a very sweet spirit. Grace, this may hurt a bit, but now is the time for you to understand about our responsibility when God whispers guidance into our hearts.

God, through his Holy Spirit, whispers into our hearts the things that are right and wrong and tells us not to do certain things that it is our responsibility when we obey or not. Your dad did not listen. This was his fault. Through your mom and Lily and myself, God is here with you now. He wants to help you to overcome this. To do that, you must not only accept what happened but allow him to help you to let it go. Allow him to help you to forgive and help you to give it over to him. He will deal with your dad. When you let it go, you release the pain of it all to him, and God's peace and joy will remain. Grace, for the moment, you need to allow yourself to accept and feel the pain of it all. You just made a huge step in remembering your past, and it will be natural to be angry, but keep God close as you do this, or it will overtake you and take you in the wrong direction. I want to see you next week, and we will talk about how you are doing and how you are dealing with it. Are you okay?"

Grace was much calmer now and answered, "Yes, and I do understand that it is his fault, but it makes me feel so dirty as if I am different from everyone else. I am angry, very angry. I was before but did not know why, and now that I do, I don't know how to get past that, but I am okay."

Jennifer, who had been sitting there quietly, spoke up, "Grace, as you take everything you are feeling to God, He will heal you and help you to feel brand-new inside. He will help you to feel like the beautiful angel within that you are inside and out. Your dad may have put 'dirty' inside, but God will take it out. He will replace it with His beauty. As he says in Isaiah 61:3, 'To bestow on them a crown of beauty instead of ashes, the oil of joy instead of mourning, and a garment of praise instead of a spirit of despair. They will be called oaks of righteousness, a planting of the Lord for the display of his splendor.'"

Marion said, "Amen!" Then Jennifer and Grace both thanked Marion, and they prayed again for the Lord to be with Grace and continue to help her through this, and then they were out the door.

As they walked to their cars, Jennifer stopped and asked, "Grace, are you going to be okay? Do you want me to come with you?"

"No, Mom," Grace answered. "I think more than anything I just need to be alone. By the way, I know I have just been saved, but I do understand that I need to forgive. I don't know how to do it right now, but I know if God has brought me this far, then he will take me the rest of the way and help me with that as well. Thank you, Mom, for coming. It meant a lot that you were here. I love you."

"I love you too, and I am glad I could be here for you. Call me if you need me," Jennifer said as they hugged each other before getting into their cars to leave.

Grace went to the park by her home that she always

Went to and sat on a bench that was secluded all by itself. She had so many emotions bubbling up inside. She did not feel disconnected from everything that had been told to her. She remembered, and it hurt. It hurt so much, and she felt as if she had lost her dad and he had just died. The pain and the anger were so great she could not hold it back anymore. She was glad that no one was in the park, and at that moment, she just started crying and screaming in anger at the same time, "Why, why, Daddy! Why did you hurt me like that? Why! I want to hate you, but I can't! Why did you do that to me? Why, why, why did you do it?

She prayed aloud: "Oh Lord, I know I need to let go and forgive. I understand what it means to forgive, that it is releasing me from the hold of my abusers. I do get it, Father, that as long as I hold on to bitterness and resentment and do not forgive the ones who hurt me, they are still controlling and hurting me. They are hurting me by the pain and anger that I will not release, but I am so angry! Show me how and help me. I just can't right now because I am so angry. Please help me."

Grace sat there and cried and cried, and she did not even see Christine.

The kindly little old lady walks up and sits beside her. Christine sat there beside her and just held her as if she knew what Grace was crying about. She just sat there and held her. That was what Grace needed; she just needed to be held and to be loved—unconditionally loved. She needed love to push all the pain and anger she felt away.

Christine just sat there and held her for a while. Then she gently took Grace's face in her hands. She said in a soft voice, "My dear, you are wondering how to forgive those who have hurt you. It is a choice. It is something that you choose to do first and speak it. Your heart will hear. And as you keep speaking it even though your heart may not line up at the moment, as long as you keep it in your mind to forgive, your heart will eventually. Decide in your mind first that you want to be free. Then all you have to do is speak it. It is like faith. 'Faith comes by hearing and hearing the Word of God.' Just speak it my child, and your heart will eventually line up."

Grace looked at her and smiled. She knew that she was sent here by God, and the love this little old lady was showing her was calming her heart. She thought she must be an angel.

Then Grace spoke, "Oh yes, I do want to let go, and I do want to forgive. I don't want to feel all this pain anymore. The abuse and the anger have taken so many years from me already, and I do not want to give them any more."

Christine sat there a moment longer and just held her. Then she started singing silently, *Peace be still your broken heart and let His peace flow through. Let it flow. Let it flow. Like a river throughout, let it flow. Peace be still in your broken heart.*

All of a sudden, Grace felt like a cool rain had swept through her heart. She knew it was from God. He was helping her and teaching her how to forgive.

She looked over at Christine and said, "I am ready now." Then she looked up toward heaven and said, "Father, I choose to forgive my dad and Bobby for hurting me. I forgive them for the abuse they inflicted upon me, and, Father, whenever our faces meet again, I even pray, please help me to let go and forgive again, in Jesus's name, amen."

Right at that moment, Grace knew she would be all right. The fight that had been going on within her for so long seemed to vanish, and the sweetest peace filled her spirit.

Grace looked over at Christine and said, "Thank you, thank you so much. I needed this. I needed to be held and loved. I needed the love that you have shown to make the hurt go away. God must have sent you just for me."

Christine smiled and said, "He did, my child, and he has orchestrated every step you have taken to lead you straight to him and to his saving Grace and the healing and deliverance it brings. He loves you, dear Grace, more than you may ever know, and you are his princess. Don't ever forget that, and don't ever let anyone make you feel any different."

Grace smiled and sat there a little while longer, with her head on Christine's shoulder as if she was a little girl again. She knew there would still be emotions within to battle and to conquer, but now she knew how. Just open up your mouth when troubles come and call on the Father and the One, who died in her stead. He was there for her now, and she knew he would be there for her again.

The Spirit of the Lord God is upon me, because the Lord has anointed me to bring good news to the afflicted; He has sent me to bind up the brokenhearted, To proclaim liberty to captives and freedom to prisoners; to proclaim the favorable year of the Lord and the day of vengeance of our God; to comfort all who mourn, to grant those who mourn in Zion, giving them a crown of beauty instead of ashes, the oil of gladness instead of mourning, a garment of praise instead of a spirit of despair. So they will be called oaks of righteousness, the planting of the Lord, that He may be glorified.

—Isaiah 61:1–3

9

Healing Begins

Grace was so excited! Jolisa was coming, and she would be there tomorrow. She was busy with making sure the guest rooms were fixed just right. Every room had a beach theme with varied colors of blue and blue-green. She was going into town today to get some fall-colored leaves and cinnamon-scented pinecones to decorate the living and dining room.

She bought a huge turkey and all the fixings! She was not as good of a cook as her mother or even Lily and relied heavily on their help. Lily was coming up as well. She was going to stay through the weekend. It was going to be fun! She had not seen either of them in about a year. She had been very busy with work. The magazine had her traveling a lot in the past year, but she did not mind it. Grace loved nature and loved even more capturing it on film. She even brought some of the pictures to life again on canvas. Grace loved her job, but painting was her heart's devotion.

"Good morning, Mr. Henry!" Grace shouted as she began her morning walk. "How are you this morning? My sister will be here tomorrow, and I am so excited! You are still coming to Thanksgiving dinner, aren't you?" A big smile suddenly appeared on his face.

He replied as Sissy came up to Grace, wagging her tail, as if Sissy knew they were talking about food.

"Of course, especially since I will not have to cook! How can I pass that up? By the way, how is your sister? Did she ever graduate?"

"Oh yes, and she is working as an RN at Lexington Medical Center in Columbia. She has hours that are varied and never the same, but she really likes it. I can't wait to see her," Grace answered.

Walking on with Sissy wagging her tail happily right beside him, Mr. Henry said, "I will be glad to see her as well. You two are like the granddaughters I never had."

Grace gave him a huge smile and said, "Thank you. You know we love you too. You are family to us," and then she waved at him as she walked on by continuing down the beach.

Grace was going to cut her walk short this morning. She had so much to do to get ready for everyone. Her mind was rolling over everything she needed to buy from town. She did not want to make two trips even though she was sure there would be things her mom would want once she and Sam arrived. She had grown to love Sam and loved him as if he were a father to her. As she walked her mind drifted back to that time, she finally came to terms with what happened. She never expected Sam to have such an effect on her as he did. She had not been able to trust anyone and especially men, but he touched her heart, and the fatherly love he showed her was actually a stepping stone to being able to trust people again.

******

Grace took off work the day after her session with Marion and felt as if she made progress. She was in awe of the heavenly Father she had just barely met and began believing in due to the way he showed himself to her in the park through Christine, but she still hurt a lot. Marion told her to work through her emotions—to feel them but not let them carry her away and have a hold on her. It was all too overwhelming at the time to process all that she said, but now she was beginning to realize what she meant. Emotions were bubbling up within her, and all she wanted to do was cry again. This time it was different; there was no anger, just heartache. It was heartache in the way of loss. She felt as if she had lost someone she had cherished and loved for so long. She had forgiven him, but at the same time, she felt so betrayed.

Grace cried out to God, "Father, please give me the wisdom to know how to handle this pain and how to let it go." Then she rolled over in bed and put the covers over her head and cried herself back to sleep.

For the next couple of weeks, Grace was having a hard time with the feeling of loss she was experiencing. She had mentioned it to Marion in her session with her, but Marion encouraged her, saying that she had made tremendous progress. Grace kept reading the Bible and had even begun going to church with Lily. She liked it and told Lily, "I am surprised. I didn't know what to expect, but they seem like a family, and you can tell that they are sincere when they ask about you and when they pray for one another. I really like it."

They were even going to the Family Fun Night on Friday. Grace thought it would be fun. They were going to have a potluck dinner and a movie. Grace had never done anything like that before and was excited to go.

Lily could see the difference in Grace and told her, "Grace, you seem so much more at peace and happy since your sessions with Marion over the last couple of weeks. The prayer therapy worked, didn't it?"

"Well," Grace started in, "it wasn't so much the session as what happened afterward. I never told you because I was hurting so much. I finally remembered, and it felt as if it had just happened. I needed to be alone, so I went to the park. I was sitting on the bench alone and crying and doing a little screaming as well. Then all of a sudden, there appears beside me the nice little old lady I had told you about before. Lily, she just knew. I can't explain it, but by the way she sat there and held me and talked to me, she knew. She explained about forgiveness and sang a song, something like 'peace flow like a river into her heart.' When she did, it felt as if God himself came down and touched my heart. I felt an overwhelming peace sweep through my heart. It calmed me down in such a way it was as if a big bolt of love just hit my heart. It gave me the strength to say the words, 'I forgive them.' After I had said those words, the anger vanished."

By the time Grace had finished, Lily had tears running down her face and cried out, "Thank you, God. Thank you!"

The girls had a lot of fun at the Family Fun Night, and Grace told Lily that she liked that church and wanted to keep going. Lily was quite pleased because she enjoyed Grace's company, especially now that she was so much more at peace and they grew even closer, and it was as if they had known each other all their life.

******

The weeks went by, and Grace continued to read the Bible and pray. She loved her time with God and felt that she had missed out on so much not knowing him before. She had so much peace within her now and especially when she sits alone with him in her devotion times. Such a strong sense of peace filled the room, and she could feel his presence. She read through the New Testament and began reading in the Old Testament and in the Psalms. She really liked the Psalms. She could identify with so much of the emotions that David felt.

The nightmares were gone, and the monster finally had a face. God showed her how to accept what happened and give it over to him in prayer and through forgiveness. God took the pain away and the dreams with it. She finally learned that in holding onto bitterness and forgivingness, you hold onto the pain as well. She decided that being free of the pain was so much more important to her than staying mad at her dad. She believed that God would deal with her dad. She could never say that before; she could not trust anyone. The pain was gone, the anger and the walls around her heart as well. There were walls of fear that caused so much anger and pride—pride in not allowing anyone in—with the attitude of "no one is ever going to hurt me again," along with the wall of selfishness.

Tremendous heartache puts a wall of selfishness up because all you can think about is your pain and not being hurt by anyone or anything ever again, and it also keeps you from seeing the needs of anyone else. The pain you experience is so great that all you can see and deal with is your own. There was also the wall of insecurity that the abuse caused. It made her feel "worthless" and not as good as other people and did not have confidence in herself because of it. This wall might have had took a little bit longer to come down, but as she learned to trust God and see his faithfulness to her and continued in her walk with him, her eyes opened more and more. Her eyes will be opened to the beauty that is within her giving her increasing confidence. Walls keep others from hurting you, but it keeps you locked up inside like an emotional prison. It keeps the pain in and God out.

Upon being saved and the help of her therapist Marion, Lily, her mom, and Jolisa, Grace finally understood; and she was finally free of all the pain.

******

Grace's last session with Marion was finally here, and it was sort of bittersweet. She was glad that she had healed enough in her heart to a point in which she did not need the sessions any longer, but Marion had become a very dear friend as well, and she would miss talking to her. Grace had also finished her photography class, and the students were putting on a show of their work that was open to the public. Grace had been taking pictures all around town but was especially proud of the one's she had taken in the park.

"Hi, Grace! My prize pupil! How have you been this week?" Marion asked.

Grace came in and replied, "Oh, Marion, I am going to miss you!"

"Grace," Marion answered, "you can still call whenever you want, and I expect it!"

They sat down, and Grace began, "Marion, I don't believe I would have made it this far if I had not met Jesus. The Lord has truly helped me to forgive and to let go. I have been reading through the Psalms and have seen in them how David felt as he was on the run from Saul—the pain and weariness, how he prayed and gave it to God. He even praised him in the middle of his storm. It has helped me and truly blessed me, especially how God came through for him and promoted him to the palace. After our session and my time with Christine, as I told you, I still felt a lot of pain. It was a pain as if someone I loved dearly just died, and then I began to feel hurt due to the betrayal of it all. He was my dad, and he hurt me and stole so many years from me. Then it hit me. He hurt me and stole a lot of years from me. He did this by the continued heartache and anger I felt. Now that I know and have accepted what happened in the past and have forgiven him, I don't have to let him steal the rest of my years by holding onto more pain due to it, even though it is different.

I do believe God has helped with that because of what I had prayed. I asked him to give me wisdom, and he did. It took a while, but I was finally able to let it go, and now I am so happy! Oh, by the way, my photography class is finished! We are having an exhibition of our work next week. Will you come?"

Marion was smiling from ear to ear. "Of course! I wouldn't miss it! I am so proud of you, and I feel I can now say that this is truly your last session, but please call if you ever need to talk again, and remember to continue to keep your journal. When emotions arise that you cannot deal with, remember to write down what you were doing and what you were thinking of at the time. Ask yourself why you were feeling that particular way, and it will help to deal with it and get past it."

Grace and Marion hugged, and then Grace went out the door with a huge smile on her face. She had come so far and felt so happy she could hardly believe it herself.

******

The night was finally here—the photography exhibit her teacher had put together. It was even advertised! Grace was excited and a little nervous.

"Lily, what if no one likes my pictures? There are so many students in that class who take wonderful pictures."

Lily looked over at Grace with a look of surprise and said, "Grace, have you ever really looked at your pictures? They are beautiful, and they look as if a professional photographer took them. When I look at your pictures, especially of the ones you took in the park, they make me feel as if I am right there in the park looking at the scene for myself! You have no worries and wait and see. Other people will say the same thing! Are your mom and Sam coming?"

Grace replied, "Oh yes, and even Jolisa! I thought Jolisa was scheduled to work, but she was able to trade days with someone. I am so glad they are coming, and I wonder who else will be there. My instructor advertised it. So, it will be open to the public as well. I guess that is why I am a little nervous. I enjoy taking pictures just for my pleasure, but I do want people to like them."

"Trust me," Lily answered, "they will. Your pictures are absolutely wonderful!"

The girls finished getting ready, and Grace looked stunning! Grace came out of the room wearing an aquamarine dress that accentuated her long and wavy brunette hair and brown eyes. Lily could not believe how beautiful she looked.

"Where did you get that dress?" Lily asked.

"I just bought it. I was saving it for tonight and wanted to surprise you. Do you really like it?" Grace asked. "Grace, you look like a picture out of a fashion magazine!

I love it!" Lily answered.

Lily and Grace got there a little before the showing. Grace wanted to make sure all her pictures were set up just right. Lily was surprised at all the shots. She had not realized just how many pictures Grace had taken. Grace had taken pictures of downtown Columbia and the Gervais St. Bridge. She had taken it at night, and the old-fashioned lights that went across the bridge were all lit up. Lily couldn't believe how professional it looked. She had taken close-ups of birds from the park and captured the colors of their feathers exquisitely.

Lily couldn't believe her eyes and asked Grace, "How could you ever doubt yourself? Grace, your pictures are awesome! I would buy them myself and at any price! I have seen some of your pictures and loved them, but until now I had not realized just how good you are! You do not have anything to worry about."

Grace began to blush and said, "Oh, Lily, thank you so much! You don't know how much that means to me! Oh, here comes my instructor, Mr. James. I want to introduce you. Mr. James, I want you to meet my adopted sister, Lily. Not really adopted legally, but my whole family sort of grafted her in, and she has been like a sister to me."

Mr. James looked over at Lily and smiled and said, "I am very happy to meet you, and I must admit Grace has surprised me with her work. Her pictures are excellent, and before the night is over, she just might be in store for a surprise." He excused himself and went off to greet more students and guests as they had just begun entering the room.

Jennifer, Sam, and Jolisa finally arrived and made their way over to Grace and Lily. They all stood there in awe and in unison said, "Grace, why didn't you tell us you were so good? These pictures are wonderful. They look so professional."

Jennifer continued, "Grace, I am so proud of you!"

Grace walked over and hugged her mom.

"Thank you, and it means so much to me to have you all here. I am glad the class is over now. I will enjoy the time off, and my art classes are over as well. I haven't had much time to paint, but that is where my heart lies."

Sam, who had been rather quiet, stepped up and said, "Grace, you may not be blood of my blood, but all the same you are my daughter. I am so proud of you, and in fact, if you are selling, I want the bridge picture. It will look great in my office!"

He then stepped over and gave her a fatherly smile and hugged her and said, "I love you."

Grace was taken by surprise because that was the first time since Bobby that any man had touched her, and she was even more surprised that she didn't flinch; she usually did. She was actually comforted by it, oddly enough. He wasn't her real dad, but at that moment, his genuine affection made her feel as if he was, and she looked up at him with the same affection.

She said, "I love you too, and I may not be your blood, but I am proud to be your daughter."

By that time, everyone had tears in their eyes and more so by the leaps and bounds Grace had made emotionally.

Lily could hardly believe what she had seen in Grace in allowing Sam to hug her and silently prayed, *Thank you, Father, for healing Grace's broken heart in such a wonderful way. Amen.*

Jolisa had to change the mood and asked, "Okay, this is an exhibit, and with all exhibits, there is food. So, where is the food?"

They all laughed, and Grace Spoke up, "Actually, there is food. Mr. James has a table set up on the other side of the room. Please help yourself. I want to stay here by my station."

Lily and Jolisa, talking amongst themselves, started off to the food table, while Sam and Jennifer stayed behind looking at all of Grace's pictures.

Then all of a sudden, Mr. James came walking over with a man who looked to be in his forties and he was dressed in a very expensive-looking suit. Mr. James introduced him by name only and not the business he represented.

"Grace, this is Mr. Johnson, and he wanted to meet you."

Grace walked up to him, and with a bashful smile, she said, "Good evening, Mr. Johnson. I am very happy to meet you. This is my mom, Jennifer, and my stepfather, Sam Morris."

They all shook hands, and looking at Grace's photographs in pure amazement, Mr. Johnson asked Grace, "How long have you been taking pictures?"

Grace answered, "Only for as long as I have been taking this class."

Mr. Johnson began again, "Ms. Thompson, your pictures look as if you have been doing this for years! I have photographers working for me who have been doing this for years and have not been able to capture the quality and beauty of yours. They make you feel as if you are right there. Would you mind stepping over here to talk privately with me for a moment?"

He motioned to a private place in the room, and Grace agreed, leaving her mom and Sam by themselves.

Mr. Johnson smiled and said, "Grace, your pictures have a professional quality to them and look as if you have been doing this for years. Every one of your pictures has the same quality, and you have a gift and talent that I cannot pass up. You truly have an eye for a great picture. Would you consider coming to work for me?"

Grace replied, "Where do you work, and what would I be doing?"

Mr. Johnson answered, "I own a travel magazine, and you would be one of my photographers. You would be traveling to different areas depending on what each issue is focusing on and would be taking the pictures needed for it. We would pay you a salary plus travel expenses. There is a catch, though. We are based closer to Conway and Myrtle Beach. Would that be a problem?"

Grace was in a state of shock; she certainly did not see that coming and was still speechless. Grace was trying to grasp the words to answer him. Then she began laughing, and finally, she spoke up and said, "Mr. Johnson, forgive my state of shock right now and forgive my laughter, but right before the exhibit, I was talking to my roommate and was nervous that my pictures would not be as good as the other students, which is the reason for my laughter."

Mr. Johnson started laughing as well and said, "Ms. Thompson, your pictures are more than good, and you honestly do not have any worries."

Grace, a little more composed, replied, "Mr. Thompson, I would be honored to accept your offer, and I have always loved the beach. So moving there is definitely not a problem!"

Mr. Thompson and Grace shook hands. He gave her his card and told her to call him next week to discuss more details, and then he excused himself and went over to talk to Mr. James before leaving.

Still trying to grasp what had just happened and right on cue as if it were planned, Grace's boss walked in and spotted her. They caught eyes, and she waved him over to her station. By that time, Jolisa and Lily had also come back, and they were all waiting anxiously for Grace to find out what she and Mr. Johnson were talking about. Grace walked up and introduced Brent.

"Brent, this is my mom, Jennifer, and my stepfather, Sam Morris. And this is my younger sister, Jolisa."

They all greeted one another, and Brent stood there in complete amazement while he stared at Grace's pictures.

He began, "Grace, I had no idea you were this good. These pictures are great, and you really should be doing this professionally."

Grace could not help herself. She started laughing the moment he said that, and they were all looking at her, wondering what was so funny.

Finally, after she composed herself, she said, "I am so sorry, but right before you came in, Brent, my instructor, Mr. James, brought a man over to see my work. His name is Mr. Johnson, and I have just finished talking to him about... are you ready? About a job offer! Can you believe it? A job offer. He owns a travel magazine and wants me to come and work for him as one of his traveling photographers! Oh, Brent, I am so sorry to tell you like this, but it seemed as good a time as any. I said yes! They are going to pay me salary and expenses, and he even said that I was better than some of his employees who had worked for him for years and that I had an eye for a great picture. I can hardly believe it!"

They were all in a state of shock. They all thought her pictures were excellent, but no one saw this coming, and it was Lily who spoke up first, "Grace, I am so happy for you. You sincerely deserve this, but I have an important question for you. Where is the office located?"

Hesitantly, Grace answered, "Well, that is the thing. I would have to move. The office is between Conway and Myrtle Beach, and as much as I would hate to leave you all, I do love the beach, and I cannot pass up this opportunity.

So it looks like I am moving. I have to call him next week to discuss the details further. I can't believe this. It has all happened so suddenly, but, Mom, you know I have always loved the beach, and we can visit it some other time."

Jolisa hugged Grace with tears rolling down her eyes. "Grace, we just got reunited, and now you are leaving, but even so, I am so happy for you. You do deserve this, and it will be a new beginning, and it seems to fit. It goes along with the new beginning you have made emotionally and spiritually. I am proud of you. God is giving you back the life that was stolen from you! He is so good!"

Lily walked up and hugged her as well and said, "You haven't even left, and I miss you already! I do agree with Jolisa. You deserve this. Go for it!"

It was Brent's turn now. "Grace, we have all been through so much with you. You are like family, and considering what Bobby put you through and although I am sad to see you go, I am so happy for you! Congratulations! Let me know when your last day at work will be after you talk to Mr. Johnson, and whatever you need to do is okay."

He shook hands with everyone and left.

Finally, it was Jennifer's turn. "I know it may be a week or two before you leave, but we are going to all have to get together. Grace, I am so happy for you, and to see the look of pure joy that is radiating from you right now makes up for the pain in my heart of you moving away. At least it will only be a few hours away. Count on us to come for vacation a lot! It will save us lots in hotel costs!"

They all laughed and agreed. The night finally ended, and Lily and Grace gathered up her pictures, and before leaving, she walked up to Mr. James.

"Thank you so much for inviting Mr. Johnson. I am sure he told you about the job offer. I can hardly believe it. I am still processing it."

Mr. James answered, "It was my pleasure because your pictures are that good, and I was glad to see you do so well."

They shook hands, and the girls were off.

Turning in for the evening, Grace was still going over everything that happened that night, and in her spirit, it was as if she were walking on air. Grace felt as if it was all a dream. She loved taking pictures. It brought so much joy to her heart. As she lay there and thought about it, she never expected that it would turn into a career! In fact, everything had turned around, she had her mom and her sister back in her life, and although she was still fighting with her insecurities, the anger and depression were gone! Now a job offer! It seemed all too wonderful! As the night still lingered in her thoughts, she thought unexpectedly about Sam. Grace remembered his genuine concern and could feel the love of his embrace as one of gentleness. She did not expect that or even her reaction. It made her realize that maybe, just maybe, she could trust people again and that they were not all out to hurt her. It made her smile, and she closed her eyes as a peaceful rest consumed her.

******

The next week was very busy for Grace. She phoned Mr. Johnson, and he was giving her until next month to allow her time to tie things up there and find a place in Myrtle Beach. All the girls, Jolisa, Lily, and Jennifer, were going to take a trip up to Myrtle Beach, with Grace to help her find a place. Grace had lined up a few places, but there was one in particular that she wanted to see. It was a house on the beach owned by an old couple that purchased it merely as an investment, and they just happened to live next door.

Grace thought, wouldn't it be great if I could buy that house? She was especially surprised at Sam and her mom's most generous gift.

The girls got settled in at the hotel, and Grace couldn't wait to call the real estate agent. Grace took her mom aside to confirm her generous offer before she called.

"Mom, are you sure that you want to give me the down payment money? Do you have ten thousand dollars to give? I have been saving and have five thousand dollars, and though it is not that much compared to what I would need, it would probably do. Are you sure?"

Jennifer smiled and said, "Dear Grace, we are quite sure, and in fact, it was actually Sam's idea. We do have it, and it will not hurt us in the least. We have an investment account, which is doing quite well, and it came from there. Consider it a housewarming present, a congratulations present, and a birthday present wrapped up in one! Yes, my dear, I have not forgotten your birthday! You are going to turn twenty- five years old next week! So have no doubts, and that way you can use yours for what-ever other costs may arise from buying a house."

Grace was smiling from ear to ear, and tears were beginning to roll down her face. She hugged her mom and said, "Mom, thank you so much! I am so glad I have you back in my life! Thank you for the money. I accept!"

Then she hurried off to call the real estate agent and told her that she wanted to look at the beach house first.

******

They were meeting Veronica, the real estate agent, at 10:00 a.m.; so the girls, hard as it may be to have four girls rush to get ready with one bathroom, managed. As they drove up to the house, Grace was already in love with it. There was a deck that ran across the back of the house with a great view of the beach. Even though it was on the beach, there was only one house that was right next to hers, and she thought it must be the owners. There were other houses, but there was a little distance between this one and the rest. Grace liked that and was already in love with it. Grace looked at the house and already decided that she wanted it. She did not need to look any further. It had a medium-sized kitchen and living room and three bedrooms. It had a hall bathroom, and the master bedroom had one as well. It was perfect! Grace went to look for Veronica, who had stepped outside.

"I will take it! I love it!"

Veronica replied, "That is great! Let me call the owners to see if they are home while you finish signing the paperwork. I am their listing agent, so this works out great." Grace was just finishing up when Veronica came back. "Grace, the owners, Mr. and Mrs. Henry, are home, and they accept your offer, and they would like to meet you."

"Sure," Grace replied, and with that, they all walked next door.

Grace walked up to Mr. and Mrs. Henry and held out her hand to greet them. "Good morning! My name is Grace Thompson."

"Hello," they answered back, "we are very happy to meet you."

Grace introduced her mom and sister and Lily, and they talked for a little bit. They had already become fast friends. They had decided, for

Grace's sake, on a quick closing. It would be in two weeks, which was perfect for Grace. Lily and Grace had decided to move her up there at the same time and have what would be their last weekend together for a while at the same time.

Driving back, Grace was so full of ideas about what color she was going to paint the walls and the type of furniture she wanted to buy.

"Thank you so much, Mom, for the down payment. It turns out that I do need the extra because I do not have any furniture! It seems I am going to need a little of that!"

They all laughed and agreed. When they got back, Jennifer took Lily aside and wanted to secretly plan the going-away dinner and make it a surprise birthday dinner as well. Lily was busting at the seams with joy for Grace, but at the same time, she did not want to see her go. They had become so close.

******

"Grace, come on! Aren't you ready yet? Your mom is waiting for us?" Lily yelled as she was waiting for Grace to finish up in the bathroom.

Finally, Grace came out. "Okay, okay. What is your hurry? They will not start dinner without us."

Lily, trying to seem innocent, replied, "I am just starving. That is all!"

Grace answered, "Well, I'm here, so let's go!"

As they drove up to her mom's house, Grace started crying. She could not hold the tears back any longer; it had been brewing all day. She was experiencing emotions that were new to her. She was overjoyed at every-thing that had been happening, which seemed to be all at once. She was happy about having her mom and sister back in her life, and even Sam, who had just recently became more than a stepfather to her. He had become a dad, and she was actually going to miss him more than she realized. She was just beginning to really love him, love him as a dad, and it was his unconditional love he showed to her that was a stepping-stone for her to begin trusting people again and especially men. Now she was leaving, and this job opportunity was bittersweet.

As they walked through the doors, it was as expected: Jennifer and Jolisa met them with tears in their eyes and could not let them get past the entryway from hugging Grace so tightly.

Lily spoke up, "Okay, enough tears! Let's get these tears turned into laughter. Surprise, happy twenty-fifth birthday, Grace!"

Grace looked around at the streamers and balloons and Sam standing in the doorway, and, yes, the tears started again!

Wiping the tears from her eyes, Grace said, "You all did not have to do this, but even so, thank you so much!"

She looked over at Sam and ran up and hugged him. "Sam, thank you so much and even more for being the dad that I needed during this time. Thank you, and it means more than you know, and I can't wait for you to see my new house. Thank you for the down payment or birthday present! It is an awful lot, but I am so grateful for it!"

Sam looked down at her and smiled. "Grace, you are my daughter, and we have missed having you in our life over the past few years. So consider it making up for lost time."

The evening went by quickly They sang "Happy Birthday," and Jolisa and Lily both gave Grace gift cards to a home improvement store. They decided to go practical, knowing she would need that for her new house. Finally, the evening came to a close, and they all hugged and said their goodbyes.

Grace waved as she was getting into the car and said,

"You all had better come to see me at least once a month!"

They all agreed, and Grace began crying once again as they left.

******

Grace sat on her bed with the Bible in hand before she turned in for the night and started reading the book of Ruth. She couldn't put it down and thought, "Wow, Ruth did not know you existed, Lord. She lost her husband and left home to go to a land she did not know and to a people she had never met, nor did she have anything in common with them, but she found you. You gave her a new home and a new family, and most importantly, you gave her you! Lord, thank you so much because that is what you did for me. You gave me myself, you gave me my family back, and you gave me a home and a career. Lord, in giving me all of that, to top that, you gave me a dad again and a home on the beach—something that since I was a little girl has always been in my heart. Lord, you know me full well, and I feel as if you renewed me, inside and out! Thank you so much, Father!"

As Grace drifted off to sleep, she thought about her life there with Lily and knew she would miss her so much. Lily provided the way out and through that, it was the beginning of the end of all the abuse she had suffered. Lily was a gift from God, and as happy as she was about her new job and a new home, her heart already ached at the thought of leaving Lily.

She closed her eyes with tears rolling down her face and once again prayed, "Lord, thank you for Lily. I know we are not that far away and can call, but please fill the void that will be left due to not seeing her every day. You showed me your love through her, and I going to miss her so much, but even in that, Lord, I am overwhelmed at your goodness and what you have done and that brought me through. Thank you, Lord. You have carried me through this time of transition from the bondage of abuse to deliverance and a heart full of joy. Thank you, Father. I love you!"

******

Though Grace had come through so much in the last few months, there would be one more mountain for her to face. Her time of continued healing and spiritual growth would give her the strength she needed to face it. God would be with her, and as the eagle that soars through the air with ease in God's strength, Grace would be able to face it and overcome it.

Praise the Lord, my soul; all my inmost being, praise His holy name. Praise the Lord, my soul, and forget not all His benefits who forgives all your sins and heals all your diseases, who redeems your life from the pit and crowns you with love and compassion, who satisfies your desires with good things so that your youth is renewed like the eagles. —Psalm 103:1–5

10

⌘

Free at Last!

It was Thanksgiving, and there was a lot of joyful hustle and bustle going on! Everyone had decided to come a few days before Thanksgiving, and Grace was ecstatic! Mr. Henry and Sam were outside on the deck talking, and all the girls were inside. Sam loved the house and even mentioned that the colors Grace had chosen for the wall colors seemed to fit the location perfectly. All the women were busy in the kitchen getting the dinner ready, and everyone was enjoying themselves. Grace made the stuffing and started the turkey herself.

She was a little uncertain of how it would turn out and asked, "Mom, will you check my turkey before I put it in? Do you think it will turn out okay? This is the first time I have ever baked one, and I am so glad you are making your sweet potato casserole. It isn't as sweet as candied yams, and you know I really hate them. They are way too sweet!"

Jennifer smiled and said, "Grace, your turkey looked great! I think you did a fine job seasoning and preparing it. It's going to turn out real good, and as far as the sweet potatoes, they happen to be my favorite as well."

Lily had made the pies: one was pumpkin, one was cherry, and one was a key lime cheesecake. That was for Jolisa. She loved cheesecake, and Jolisa was making homemade cranberry sauce and green beans.

Lily looked over at all the food cooking, and at the smell of it all burst out. "I don't know about you all, but this kitchen smells so good my stomach is beginning to growl!"

The day was full of joy and laughter; everyone was having a great time. Grace was done with her part, so she went out to talk with Mr. Henry and Sam.

"Are you having a good time, Mr. Henry? I hope you brought your appetite!"

"Oh yes, and I haven't eaten all day. I've been saving up for this, so I hope you have enough!" he replied.

"Well," Grace began, "only if you make it to the table before Lily. She has a very big appetite for such a skinny little thing."

They all laughed, and then Grace walked over to Sam and gave him a big hug and said, "I am so glad you're here, and I love you, Dad!"

He was completely overwhelmed and overjoyed; it was the first time ever that Grace had called him that, and he welcomed it because that was how he felt about her. To Sam, she was his daughter. Viewing from the doorway, Jennifer saw and heard it all, and the tears began to flow. She could not have asked for a better Thanksgiving. The Lord has given her a family again and has healed her daughter's heart. To see her hug Sam and call him Dad was unexpected and more than she could have hoped for because it meant that Grace was whole inside and not fearful any longer.

Grace's turkey turned out perfect, and in a humorous way, she stood up and bowed. "Thank you, thank you. It was nothing really, just inborn talent!"

They all laughed and in unison grabbed a roll and started throwing them at her! Everyone sat around afterward and had desert, and most importantly, each one said what they were thankful for and blessed the Lord. It wasn't much of a surprise that everyone had the same answer. They thanked the Lord for the healing and the family restoration that He had given them. Mr. Henry also spoke up and thanked the Lord for the same thing.

He said, "I am so grateful for the love of this family and for adopting me as their grandpa because I accept. I thought that I would be lonely when my Bonnie died, but the Lord thought of everything. He may have had to take my Bonnie home, but He left me three granddaughters in her place. Thank you, God, for loving me and not forgetting about me."

******

The next few days were full of leftovers and walking the beach and, the day after Thanksgiving, shopping! You cannot have four girls in the house on a holiday and not go shopping! As the girls left, Sam and Mr. Henry were planted on the sofa in front of the television and, of course, watching football. When women go shopping, men go to the TV.

The weekend was over, and Sunday was here. They all had to pack up and leave. Grace hugged them and thanked them for coming and said, "Since we all had so much fun, I am going to host Christmas! Okay?"

In agreement, they all stuck their heads out of their cars before leaving and shouted, "Sounds good!"

Lily, of course, had to add, "Fine with me. There will be less cooking and more food!"

Grace, in between laughs, thought as Lily drove off, that is just like Lily. After they all drove off, Grace cleaned up inside and changed into her comfy clothes, her sweatpants, and socks. She went out on to the deck to enjoy the cool November air and be alone with God and her thoughts. "Lord," she began, "thank you for such a wonderful holiday. Having my family back and being your child is what made it special. Thank you, Lord."

As she sat there, her mind drifted back to when she first moved out here. She thought about how happy she was, and yet there was still something lingering in her spirit. As much as she thought she had conquered everything, even the wall of insecurity, she sensed that something more still needed to be done. The walls of insecurity came down just as Marion had told her. The answer to that was faithfully walking with the Lord, reading the Bible, staying involved in church, and spending quality time with God—praying and talking to him. It helped her to grow spiritually and get to know God more and the depths of his love for her. Reading the Word had helped to transform her thinking from living according to the ups and downs of her emotions to being steadfast and living according to the Word and walking in the promises of God found in it.

"Do not conform any longer to the patterns of this world, but be transformed by the renewing of your mind. Then you will be able to test and approve what God's will is—his good, pleasing, and perfect will" Romans 12:2.

Knowing his great love for us helps us to trust him, and it gives us confidence in whom we are as a child of the King, which tears down that wall of insecurity.

The thought that something still needed to be done continually lingered in her spirit.

She couldn't help but wonder what it was and prayed, "Father, I know there is something else as part of my healing that I need to do. I feel as if I am healed, but I hear you telling my heart that there is something else I need to do. Please show me what it is, and if strength and wisdom are needed, please provide, in Jesus's name, amen." She continued to drink in the beauty of the ocean as her mind drifted back in time.

******

Lily was driving her car up to Myrtle Beach as well since Grace was not coming back. Grace did not have a lot and had bought a few minor things here and there but no furniture. So all that she had would fit nicely in both of their cars. They concentrated on the fun of moving instead of the time between when they would see each other again. They wanted this to be fun and memories of laughter instead of tears. The drive seemed extra-long going in separate cars, but they were finally there! Grace went over to Mr. Henry's and introduced herself to him and his wife. She asked if it would be okay if she left her things at the house even though the closing and official transfer of keys was not until 3:00 p.m.

They had a couple of hours, and Grace wanted to go up to the board-walk with Lily and grab some lunch. She was famished, and she knew Lily was since Lily was always hungry. She wondered, as small as Lily was, where did she put it all? She wondered even more why she had not noticed it before and reasoned it was due to the fog she had been in mentally and emotionally. It kept her from seeing the truth about a lot of people.

Mr. Henry happily agreed, and the girls were off. Of course, Lily shouted as they came to the first restaurant they spotted, "Stop here! I am starving, and I don't want to look anymore!"

Grace could not help but laugh and said, "I knew you would say that!"

They finished their lunch and headed to the office where the closing was, and Grace was nervously excited! "I can't believe this is happening, Lily! I am really going to purchase my first house!"

Lily replied, "I am so happy for you! I am going to miss you so much, but seeing all of this happen for you makes up for it. By the way, when do you begin work?"

Grace answered, "I have two weeks before I have to report to work. I thought I would go and introduce myself and get to know where it is next week, so when I do start, I will not be totally lost. It works out great because it will give me time to go shopping for furniture and get all set up! Since tomorrow is Saturday, I thought we could do some of that if it is okay?"

"Of course it is. It will be fun! I love to shop, even if it isn't for me!" Lily replied.

They had a lot of fun that weekend, and Grace found some great deals on furniture. She still had quite a lot to get but planned on being there for a long time, so she thought, I have plenty of time to furnish the rest of the house. I am going to take my time and enjoy it."

Although they had a lot of fun, the days seemed to fly by, and it was Sunday, and Lily had to get back to Columbia.

"Grace, I am going to miss you so much!" Lily said with tears rolling down her face.

"Me too, Lily. I don't know what I would have done without you. It was through your friendship that I had the strength to leave Bobby. Now look at where I am. I owe so much to you," Grace replied, and now they were both crying and hugging each other.

"Oh," Lily began, "what are we crying for? I am just a few hours away, and we can call all the time and you better! I can't wait to hear about your first day of work!"

"Don't worry, Lily. You will be the first one I call because you are more than a friend. You are my sister,"

Grace answered.

They hugged and cried a bit more, and Lily drove away with Grace, waving as she left and the tears flowing generously. This was when Grace became fast friends with the Henrys next door. Mrs. Henry was watching as Lily drove off and decided to change the mood, so she walked over and offered to help Grace with the house. Grace gladly accepted.

"Thank you so much for your help, Mrs. Henry. I have two weeks before I start my new job, and I thought I would take the time to paint the rooms and unpack and hang pictures. Although I do not have more than most, I have acquired a great deal in the short time I have lived with Lily," Grace said.

Mrs. Henry replied, "Oh dear, please call me Bonnie."

"Okay, and thank you again for helping. It will also help me to get to know you," Grace answered.

"I don't mind a bit, and it will give me something to do, and besides, painting might be fun!" Mrs. Henry answered.

Grace and Bonnie had a great time, and it felt as if she had known her all her life. Bonnie was warm and very gentle and sweet. They talked and talked as they unpacked and began painting. They decided to paint the bedroom and living room first since they were the first two rooms Grace had bought furniture for, and it would be arriving on Monday afternoon. Grace wanted to have it ready, so she started in the bedroom, and Mrs. Henry started painting in the living room. They worked until the evening and then decided to finish up in the morning and sat on the porch and talked for a while. Grace had felt so comfortable with Bonnie that she even told her everything she had been through.

"My, but you sure don't seem as if all that has happened to you. You seem so sure of yourself—confident and secure," Mrs. Henry spoke up.

"Well," Grace began, "it has been a long road, and I had been seeing a therapist for a couple of years, and I finally had the breakthrough right before I received this job offer. It has been God and finally being able to believe in Him and trust Him that has helped to heal my heart."

"My dear, it shows. His light truly shines through you," Mrs. Henry replied.

The next day, even Mr. Henry came over to help, and they seemed as if they had been friends for years. The furniture arrived, and with the blues and greens with which Grace had painted the walls, everything blended perfectly.

Mr. Henry said, "Grace, you sure do have an eye for color. You have done quite well because the house looks beautiful!"

"Thank you so much, Mr. Henry. This is my first home, and I am so happy to be here!" Grace answered.

Grace and the Henry's did a lot together, and they were like their own little family. Grace really liked her new home, and she had furnished it beautifully. She even loved her new job and felt as if she was always meant to be a photographer. To Grace, it was more like having fun than a job.

Then, one evening as she sat out on her porch admiring the view of the ocean and the setting sun, she thought, Wow, this is so amazing! I want to capture this view on canvas. This was when she began painting, and her paintings were just as wonderful as the photographs she took. Sitting out on her deck and painting the sunsets and the sunrises gave her so much peace; it was her favorite pastime.

Grace came back to the present as she sat on her deck, looking over at the waves rolling in, and thought, it has been such a joy living here. "Thank you, Father, for all you have done and all you have brought me through."

Yet the thought of something she needed to do was lingering still in her mind, and she wondered what it could be. The thought lingered still throughout the week, you're not done yet, but Grace did not understand what it meant. Then on Friday morning, Grace received a call from her mother.

"Grace, Jolisa, and I are coming out Saturday if you don't mind. I have something I need to tell you, and I cannot do it over the phone."

Grace replied, "Mom, you are scaring me. What is it?

You are not sick, are you?"

Jennifer continued, "It is nothing like that, but it is something that I would like to tell you in person. Will you be home?"

Grace answered, "Sure, Mom, I will be home. I have a business trip to take in a couple of weeks, but for now, I will be home. I am going to Tennessee. I love it there! I am going to Pigeon Forge and Gatlinburg!"

"Wow!" Jennifer shouted. "You are going to have to share some of the pictures you take with us when we come for Christmas!"

"Sure, Mom, I would be happy to," Grace answered, "but why can't you tell me now what you have to tell me?"

"It is just something I would rather say in person if that is okay," Jennifer said.

"Okay, I will be here. Love you and see you tomorrow," Grace answered.

Grace could hardly sleep that night with thoughts of what could it be. Running through her mind. She also wondered if it had anything to do with the lingering thoughts she kept having of something still left unfinished—something she still needed to do.

Grace was waiting outside when her mom and Jolisa drove up, and it turned out that Jolisa did not know what it was either.

"Hi, Mom," Grace said as she hugged her mom.

Greeting her at the car, she said, "I am glad to see you, but I could hardly sleep last night wondering what could be so important—so important that you had to drive all this way to tell me."

Jennifer began to say, "Well, can we get something to drink and sit down inside, and I will tell you."

"Sure, Mom," Grace answered.

They all got settled in the living room; then Jennifer spoke up, "Girls, I received a phone call from your father Monday. He is getting out on parole a few years early. He wants to see you both and especially you, Grace. We talked for a while, and he said that being in prison all these years was hard but beneficial. He had to go to counseling and discovered a lot about himself and his father—things he did not realize that he had buried and forgotten. They were things that had injured his heart and soul just as yours was Grace. He even says that he has received the Lord since being in prison. They gave him a Bible, but he never wanted to read it, yet he said he couldn't throw it away either. It was not until he had been in prison for a few years and worked through all the anger he had inside and allowed the counseling sessions to help him that he decided to start reading it. He did not think he needed counseling until something the counselor said hit home so to speak and stayed on his mind until he dealt with it. It was then that he was able to start reading the Bible as well."

Jolisa and Grace sat there and listened intently and were overwhelmed. They were shocked and speechless; Grace did not know how to respond. She thought she had worked through all the fear, and then the Lord reminded her, that there is something else you need to do.

She explained this lingering thought to her mom and said, "Now I understand what it means. I think God wants me to face him and forgive him. Mom, I have to say that I am scared to do that. I don't want all those fears and emotions to sweep over me again. I do not know if I can face him and forgive him and remember all that he had done to me at the same time. How do I do that?"

Jennifer smiled and said, "Grace, you forget whom you belong to now. You are now a child of God, and you are never alone. He says, *'I will never leave you nor forsake you,'* and you do not have to do this by yourself. Do it in his strength and not yours alone. *'I can do all things through him who gives me strength,'* and he also says, *'I am the vine, and you are the branches, and apart from me you can do nothing.'"*

Grace replied, "Thanks, Mom, I needed that, and I know that is what I need to do, but I am still scared. When does he want to see us?"

Jennifer answered, "Grace, remember, courage is not the absence of fear. It is doing whatever you need to do while being afraid. He is getting out Tuesday of next week and will be getting settled in a halfway house and wants to see you Thursday if that is okay."

Grace looked over at Jolisa and then back to her mom and said, "Thanks, Mom, I needed to be reminded of that, and I know in my heart God wants me to do this, and I guess I need to do it. I do not ever want anyone or any emotion to have control over me ever again. So this is something that I need to do to have complete freedom. So I will go."

Jolisa did not have a lot to say, because she hardly remembered him, and the anger she had was in knowing what he had done to Grace and had entrusted her heart to God to help her to forgive, so she agreed as well.

Jennifer and Jolisa stayed the night and went back to Columbia the next morning.

Grace sat on the deck and drank in the beautiful sunrise and prayed, "Dear Father, I know now why you have been preparing my heart with thoughts of something I still needed to do. It was to prepare me for this so I would know you wanted me to see him and forgive him in person. You want to give me complete freedom, and I cannot turn away from it, but at the same time, Father, I am afraid. Please deliver me from my fears, and give me the strength to face him and the words to say to him, in Jesus's name, amen."

Grace went through the next few days with thoughts of meeting her father and what it would be like continually on her mind. She called Lily and told her about it. Lily agreed with her that it was something she needed to do, and if God had been preparing her in advance for it, then he would most certainly walk her through it. Grace felt a lot better after talking to her.

*****

The day was finally here, and she was driving to her mom's house, and they were meeting her father at a nearby park. Jennifer was not quite ready to have him over at her house yet. They were all a little nervous and joined hands in prayer before they left.

"Father, it is your will that we forgive and love one another. Please give us the strength to forgive and the strength to let your love shine through us and receive whatever it is he has to say, in Jesus's name, amen."

They did not know what to expect when they got to the park and did not even know what he would look like or if they would recognize him, and all at once, they spotted him. He was a lot older and with a head full of gray hair. Rough times have a way of showing through, and he did not look scary at all.

They came up to him at the same time, and Jennifer spoke first, "Mark, how are you doing?"

He had peace and yet a deep sadness in his eyes at the same time.

He looked up and said, "Hi, Jen. I am so glad to see you. Please sit down."

Grace had not spoken a word yet and was almost frozen, as she sat across from him. He told them about his parole and what he had been doing and about the abuse that he had gone through. His own father had molested him as a young boy and had buried the memory of it in his mind. When all the trouble started happening with his job in Columbia after they had moved there, the memories tried to start surfacing, and that is when the drinking got worse. He could not bear the thought of it, so he tried to cover it up in the temporary peace that alcohol gives. The only trouble with that is when the buzz wears off, the memory is still there, and you have less money in your wallet and trouble at home. It becomes a vicious cycle because the trouble at home makes you want to drink even more.

He told them that the counselor helped him to work through it. He learned that it was his disturbed way of trying to compensate for his own feelings of inadequacy by the abuse he inflicted on Grace. After he had been saved, it took a good many years for him to let go and forgive his dad, who was now passed on, and to forgive himself for what he had done to Grace. The counselor explained to him that he needed to get past the guilt, the shame, and the anger and let go. They would be walls that would keep the Grace of God's forgiveness from flowing through his heart and bringing complete healing in such a way he would be strong enough to face Grace.

The Bible says, "Forgive and you will be forgiven." He finished explaining all he had learned and discovered and looked over at Grace and asked her, "Grace, can we step aside over there for a moment alone if that is okay?" After listening so intently and being almost frozen the whole time to all that he had been through, she felt peace like a river instantly flowing through her whole spirit, and Grace knew it was God. He was telling her that he was with her and would help her to see this through. Grace agreed, and they walked over to another nearby bench in eyes distance of Jolisa and her mom. As they watched, Mark began to ask Grace to forgive him.

"Grace, I know the words I am sorry to seem so small in comparison to what I put you through and how I violated not only your body but your spirit. I am sorry, and if could go back and change it and take it away, I would. Please forgive me, and allow me to make it up to you if at all possible."

Grace sat there a moment, and before she knew it, the words seemed to flow from within. "I do forgive you, and it is only by the Grace of God that I can. I received Jesus as Lord and Savior a few years ago, and he has walked me through a healing process that has taken away all my pain. I had a lot not only from you but from my now ex-husband. After what you had done, I buried it as well, and the feeling of being ugly inside me made me feel as if I was never as good as anyone else. I felt I did not deserve anyone who would treat me right, and I ended up marrying someone who was very controlling and who abused me physically. I had a lot to overcome, but through a very good friend and her help and guidance that the Lord brought into my life, I was able to get the courage to leave him. He is now in jail for what he did to me. It was through all of that and a few more 'God moments'—things that could only happen by God himself—that I finally met Jesus and asked him into my heart. He walked me through the process of healing my heart and bringing me to the point that I am stronger within than even I thought.

I was scared to come here today. I didn't know how I would feel, and I had been delivered from fear and anger and did not want it back. After hearing you, although it doesn't make it right, because everyone has a choice, I do understand. Hurting people, if not helped and healed by God, will hurt other people by all the pain and anger they have inside controlling them just like it controlled me all those years. God has healed my heart and has been preparing me for this moment. He has been telling me,

'There is something else you need to do,' and I know this is what he meant. Dad, I do forgive you, and I can say in all honesty, I love you. It is only by and through God that I can say that because I know he loves me and is with me, and he loves you as well, which is why he wanted me to forgive you."

They sat there a few moments more and talked, and before making their way back over to Jennifer and Jolisa, they stood there and hugged each other. They both began crying. As she cried and hugged her dad, Grace felt a peace sweep through her body that she had never felt before; she had felt the Lord's peace many times, but this was different. This time, it was as if she was lighter than air.

Her mom and Jolisa watched as they hugged. Jennifer knew there would be more apologies to be made to them. But to see her little girl finally healed in such a way that she could hug her abuser—the one who stole so many years of her life through the pain of it—was heartwarming.

Jolisa and Jennifer looked at each other with eyes that seemed to say, if Grace can forgive him, we can too. Before long, they were all crying—crying tears of joy, tears of forgiveness, and tears of freedom.

As Grace stood there in her father's arms, still hugging him and still crying, she silently prayed, *Thank you, Father. God. I don't know why it took me so long to find you and to discover the joy in forgiving and the joy of giving my pain to you and learning to trust you, but thank you, Father, for waiting on me. Thank you, Father, for the people you placed in my life to lead me to you and to your saving Grace. My heart is whole, and now my family is too. I now understand the freedom of Grace and the freedom that forgiveness brings to your heart. I am free at last, and my heart is overwhelmed with joy! My heart feels lighter than air—as if I can ride the wind, the winds of your love. Thank you, Father, for your overwhelming love.*

"But for you who fear my name, the Sun of righteousness will rise with healing in its wings; and you will go forth and skip about like calves from the stall. You will tread down the wicked, for they will be ashes under the

soles of your feet on the day which I am preparing," says the Lord of hosts. Malachi 4:2–3.

Trust God for yourself. Dare to believe, and let him carry you. Ride the winds of his love and his saving Grace. It is in the broken wings of humility that you find everything. You find the Father, and his healing love will consume your heart, bringing you peace and joy within. You will not lose anything by giving him a chance, and you just might gain everything!

Broken Wings

With broken wings, I worship you. You give me strength and in my spirit your
Grace flows through.
Fly high! Fly high!
With broken wings, fly high!
Fly high! My spirit sings! Fly high! Fly high! With broken wings.
If Jesus Christ is your King,
You'll know the song my spirit sings! Fly high! Fly high!
With broken wings, fly high!
Fly high! My spirit sings! Fly high!
Fly high, up through the skies.
Sing the joy my Savior brings.
Fly high! Fly high!
My voice is raised, fly high!
Fly high! Fly high!
With broken wings, fly high!
Fly high! My spirit sings!
The Savior reigns!
Up on His throne so high, Fly high!

Carry Me

Carry me when my trials overwhelm me and my load gets too much to bear. I run to You and seek Your face; Your love is always there.

I will worship You and seek your saving Grace. I will worship You and always seek Your face.

Surrendered to Your love, I'm carried by Your Grace. Your strength holds me up; Your love will never fail or forsake.

Carry me, O Lord; I'm surrendered to Your mercy and Your Grace. Carry me, O Lord; Your love will hold me up, and the forgiveness through Your blood has given my heart a new face.

Carry me, O Lord, through life's hills and valleys, good times and bad. Carry me, O Lord. I'm surrendered to Your Grace.

In repentance, all my sins are erased. Your glory I will always seek because I'm surrendered to your Grace.

Carry me, O Lord, into the heights of the heavens above and into the depths of your love. Surrendered to Your will; I'm carried by Your Grace. Your strength holds me up and Your love will never fail or forsake.

Carry me, O Lord, I'm surrendered to Your Grace. I will worship You and always seek Your face.

I Died Today

You carry me, lifeless in Your hands. I am dead to the world and to my flesh that You may live free in me.
I have fought and wrestled against the struggles in my heart, wanting all the pain to be free from me.
The answers to my pain You already knew. There was only one thing that I needed to do.
Yet I struggled on, trying in my own way and praying in desperation. The fight continued on; my heart truly broken, I cry out, "Please, God, show me Your way!"
You knew the way and were patient with my stubborn heart, fighting for its own way and failing to see it Yours.
Weary from the pain and the trials that wore me out, I fall lifeless into Your hands.
The path has broken my heart. I finally died today. My will inside me gone.
It's buried with my pain, and in Your hands, I lay. My heart cries out, "I'm tired, Lord. There's no more fight. My heart struggles no more."
To my amazement, the peace I sought finally came. When to my will I died and I called to You and gave myself. My heart will never be the same.
That was the way all along. For God is great, and His way is best. We must die to self and seek His Grace; in us, let His glory be revealed that we may see His face.
He'll wait patiently to hear us say, "Lord, not my will, but Thy will be done." His peace will come, and You will never be the same. When in Your heart His presence known, You will shine;
His glory known in Jesus's name.

Redeeming Eyes of Love

I have walked the road of heartache and pain and gave my heart away somewhere along the way.

The roads I've traveled since are many; some were bitterness and anger, some were self-pity, and others forgivingness. In giving it away, numbness filled my heart.

Yet through all the clutter and walls that I myself erected round my heart, you still loved and saw me with Your Redeeming Eyes of Love.

You placed an angel on my path that saw right through my self-made walls. She looked at me with Your Redeeming Eyes of Love and led me straight to you.

I let you in and gave my heart to you; though I thought my heart was lost, you had it all along. I hold the key to let you in, and you hold the key to make it new again.

My story is not over; a new path I needed to begin with roads paved with love and restoration created for me before time began.

Each road is hard and involves a process of tearing down my self-made walls. With each step I take and each road I walk, a wall comes tumbling down.

Now, instead of walls around my heart, the tree of life grows there. My heart was never lost to you, and the love in Your Redeeming Eyes has replaced the heartache and pain with joy and fullness of life!

God Loves You!

I have loved you with an everlasting love; I have drawn you with loving-kindness.
—Jeremiah 31:3

"God our Savior, who wants all men to be saved and to come to the knowledge of the truth" *—1 Timothy 2:3-4*

He will not knock on the door of your heart forever. Will you let Him in?

"Here I am! I stand at the door and knock. If anyone hears my voice and opens the door, I will come in and eat with him, and he with me" *—Revelation 3:20.*

Jesus is the only way to God.

"I am the way, the truth, and the life. No one comes to the Father except through me" *— John 14:6.*
"I tell you the truth, no one can see the kingdom of God unless he is born again" *— John 3:3.*

And you must make Him Lord of your life.

"No one can serve two masters" *—Matthew 6:24.*
"Not everyone who says to Me, 'Lord, Lord', will enter the kingdom of heaven, but only he who does the will of My Father who is in heaven" *—Matthew 7:21.*

We must leave our old ways behind.

"If a house is divided against itself, that house cannot stand" *——Mark 3:25.*

You can't live according to the flesh and desires of the sinful nature and expect to have Jesus in your heart. He is holy. He is love. Love and Hate cannot exist together.

"You were taught, with regard to your former way of life, to put off your old self, which is being corrupted by its deceitful desires; to be made new in the attitude of your minds; and to put on the new self, created to be like God in true righteousness and holiness" —*Ephesians 4:22–24.*

God gives you the ability to do His will. He knows it is hard.

"I can do everything through Him who gives me strength" —*Philippians 4:13.*
"For all have sinned and fall short of the glory of God" —*Romans 3:23.*
"If we confess our sins, He is faithful and just and will forgive us our sins and purify us from all unrighteousness" —*1 John 1:9.*
"Yet to all who received Him, to those who believed in His name, He gave the right to become children of God" —*John 1:12.*
"For it is with your heart that you believe and are justified, and it is with your mouth that you confess and are saved" —*Romans 10:10.*

Then after you confess and ask forgiveness and receive Jesus into your heart, you must testify (tell someone) and be baptized. In this, God is glorified, and others might be saved by your example.

"So do not be ashamed to testify about our Lord" —*2 Timothy 1:8.*
"And this water symbolizes baptism that now saves you also not the removal of dirt from the body but the pledge of a good conscience toward God. It saves you by the resurrection of Jesus Christ" —*1 Peter 3:21.*

Special Invitation

I cannot close this book without giving you the awesome privilege of becoming a child of God, a chance to have every wrong made right and every sin washed away. If you have never asked Jesus into your heart—or maybe you did, but you were never sincere—please pray this prayer. It will be the best thing you have ever done.

After you do this, find a good church to go to if you do not have one already. Fellowshipping with other Christians will help you on your new walk in Christ. It is also a place to worship God and learn more about Him. Also, tell someone! You must confess! This should be the happiest day of your life because you now know that your eternal home is in heaven!

I think that is the best life insurance anyone can have, and it is free!

"That if you confess with your mouth, 'Jesus is Lord,' and believe in your heart that God raised Him from the dead, you will be saved. For it is with your heart that you believe and are justified, and it is with your mouth that you confess and are saved" *Romans 10:9–10.*

Congratulations, and welcome to the family of God!

Invitation to Salvation Prayer

Dear Almighty Father in heaven, I know that I am a sinner, and I ask your forgiveness of all my sins. I want to make you the Lord of my life, and I want to serve you all the days of my life. I believe that Jesus Christ died on the cross for my sins.

Thank you so much for loving me and waiting on me to come to the knowledge of the truth! Thank you for my salvation. Please help me and guide me in learning your Word so I can be a light to the world.

Please, Jesus, come into my heart and baptize me with your Holy Spirit. I thank you and praise your holy name and ask all this in the name of Jesus Christ, our Lord. Amen.

Hotline Numbers

If you have been the victim of abuse, here are a few numbers that may be of assistance to you:

1. National Suicide Prevention Lifeline Call 24/7: 1-800-273-8255 http://www.suicidepreventionlifeline.org
2. National Domestic Violence Hotline 1-800-799-7233 or TTY 1-800-787-3224 http://www.thehotline.org
3. National Child Abuse Hotline 1-800-4-A-CHILD (1-800-422-4453) http://www.childhelp.org/programs/type/hotline
4. National Sexual Assault Hotline 1-800-656-HOPE(4673) http://www.rainn.org/get-help/national-sexual- assault-hotline

Sources

Legal information were supplied from the following:

Law Offices of James R. Snell Jr. LLC 316 South Lake Dr., Lexington, SC 29072

Psychological information supplied by

Christian counselor Sister Kimberly Marie Hartfield Go Fish Ministries Inc. with a master's degree in psychological counseling assists with cases of childhood sexual abuse, Christian counseling, domestic violence and rape, sexual violence
Website: http://gofishministries.wordpress.com
Sister care Inc.
By permission of Director Nancy Barton
PO Box 1029
Columbia, SC–29202 Phone: 803.926.0505
Crisis line: 803.765.9428

Note: Each case is different, and how each person is helped is dependent on a number of factors. There are a lot of factors that go into determining how to proceed in helping victims of emotional, verbal, physical, and sexual abuse. Do not confront your abuser unless directed by the Lord. Only God knows when the right time will be to do that—if and when He wants you to.

Other Books By Sandra Lott

Adult Books

Jeremy's Journey
Safe In Papa's Hands
Her Final Curtain
Deep Waters Within
Deep Waters Rage: Sequel to Deep Waters Within
The Train Ride: One Woman's Journey
My Father's Eyes: Seeing Yourself Through The Eyes of Love
Hannah: From Barren to Blossom
An Eagle's Flight
A Princess in Waiting
The Princess in the Harlot
God's Love
Step By Step Into A Deeper Walk In Christ
I'm Saved! Where Do I Go From Here?
The Day Hope Was Born: God's Gift of Love
The Holy Spirit and the Baptism of the Holy Spirit
Repairing Broken Walls: Restoring Joy & Peace-The Book
Repairing Broken Walls: Restoring Joy & Peace-The Study Guide
Jewels From the Word & Manna For the Soul
Captivated By God's Love: Poems From the Heart
You've Got This: Learning To Let Go
I'm Saved! What Next? Beginning Your Walk In Christ
Abide In Me: A Seven-Week Study On The Blessings Of Being In God's Presence

Children's Books

The Sheep That Went Astray
Naomi's Joy
Molly's Journey to Forgiveness
Tim & Gerald Ray Series: The Wind Has a Voice
Tim & Gerald Ray Series: How Did He Get in There?
Tim & Gerald Ray Series: A Light in the Sky
Tim & Gerald Ray Series: Let's Go Swimming
Tim & Gerald Ray Series: Blowing in the Wind
Tim & Gerald Ray Series: Summer on Grandma's Farm
Sassy Goes Exploring

Sandra Lott was born and raised in San Antonio, Texas, with one sister and two brothers. Sandra loves the mountains, making candles, and jewelry.   She is the author of Jeremy's Journey, Deep Waters Within, A Princess in Waiting, Ride the Wind, and more. She has also written children's such as, The Wind Has a Voice and How Did He Get in There, Molly's Journey to Forgiveness, and more. She has written over 34 books to date and began writing poetry as soon as she was saved in June 1998. The Lord gave her, her first book to write right after her son was killed. Writing was not something she sought out. She poured her heart into time spent with the Lord in order to allow Him to heal her heart and the name of her first book was birthed in her spirit along with the chapters and what it was to be about during a devotion time. It was called: God's Love; ironically enough, with all that she was going through, God's love was exactly what she needed.

She is passionate about studying the Bible. She has taught Sunday school, and Bible Study Groups, and has been actively serving in her present church, served in the Celebrate Recovery Ministry, and Homeless Outreach. Sandra was also interviewed on radio shows such as Golden Life Living and WMAP Radio (World's Most Amazing People based out of New York), the Bill Martinez show and a Fox Radio show called the Kim Kennedy Show.

She is a devoted mother of 2 sons (Tim & Gerald Ray), Gerald Ray the youngest, has gone on to be with the Lord due to a car accident. Through the death of her youngest son at the age of 16, a rocky marriage to an alcoholic and the abuse that came with that, and other overwhelming trials, she has drawn close to the loving arms of the Father. Experiencing God's unconditional love as He held her heart in His hands, has created a passion in her to help others grow in their understanding of and receive God's love and grow spiritually. She has the heart to help hurting women discover the princess in Christ that they truly are and overcome abuse. She teaches on topics to help you reach spiritual maturity, persevere through the hard times, and how to reach your destiny in Christ!